Also by Carl Dane:

Hawke and Carmody Western Novels

Valley of the Lesser Evil

Canyon of the Long Shadows

Rage under the Red Sky

Rapid Fire Reads (short books)

Delta of the Dying Souls

The Mountain of Slow Madness

ISBN: 9781794036840

RAGE

UNDER THE

RED SKY

A HAWKE & CARMODY WESTERN NOVEL

CARL DANE

RAGING BULL PUBLISHING

Dedication

To Cathy, Mark, and Carl.
With love.

Chapter 1

Aman holding a revolver a foot away from my nose can't react to my movement and fire faster than I can swat the gun away.

That was my theory, anyway, and I hoped it would hold up because it looked like I would have no alternative but to test it. Hollis Carpenter was convulsing with rage or fear or some other emotion I could not explain at the moment. His entire body was quaking, and that included the hand holding the Smith and Wesson, a sleek two-tone .44 that I'd come to admire, though not necessarily from the present angle.

Carpenter's thumb turned a little white under the nail, the tell-tale that he was pressing down on the hammer and I was in imminent danger of having most of my head detached from my body.

I dislike the idea of dying as much as the next man, but I am particularly opposed to that fate when I don't understand the motive behind it. I knew Carpenter was something of a slimy creature – I'd deposited him in my local iron bar hotel a few times for theft, and he was from a large family of criminals who infested a broad swath of my little slice of

Texas Hill Country – but I hadn't come to arrest him or cause him any trouble.

In fact, the only reason I'd appeared at his doorstep was to return his watch, or at least a watch that was engraved "HC." I couldn't think of anyone else with those initials within a day's ride of Shadow Valley, so on the way back from serving a warrant a few miles north I took a short detour and in the process verified another of my theories – that no good deed goes unpunished.

I had the watch in my hand when he came to the door. I was going to explain that I'd found it while cleaning up the aftermath of the weekly brawl at the Silver Spoon, the bar and bordello owned by my girlfriend, Elmira Adler. I knew that Carpenter hadn't been there, and I assumed it had been stolen from him and dropped by the thief during the melee, and I was going to say as much. But I never had a chance.

Carpenter spotted the watch and in quicksilver instant his lips drew back and he snarled with a mouthful of teeth as yellow and stubby as kernels of corn. He opened the door a few more inches to expose the gun he'd been holding in his right hand and then stuck it in my face.

The man certainly was on edge. Maybe it was the strange electricity in the air.

I could feel it, too: a sensation like ants on my skin, and in between the rumbles of thunder there were brittle snapping sounds in every direction and the air was sharp with that coppery smell you detect right before a lightning strike.

And then a bolt of lightning snaked across the scarlet morning sky to my left, low, maybe a couple miles away, and I knew there would be a violent crack of thunder in a second or two, maybe loud and sudden enough to push him over the edge.

So that's when I struck.

I brought up my left hand and wiped it from right to left across my face, knocking the barrel aside, and I grabbed the body of the revolver with my right.

In a situation like that you never try to tug or wrestle because you're likely to make the gunman shoot you whether he wants to or not. Instead, you bend the gun back against his fingers, which causes a great deal of pain and puts the business end of the weapon in worrisome proximity to your opponent's face, giving him a powerful incentive to let loose.

Of course, that assumes your opponent's brain is functioning. Carpenter's mind was apparently the size of a raisin and functioning at the level of a raging reptile. He responded, against all normal human instincts, by clenching tighter as I twisted harder.

The thunderclap was concussive, like the wave that hits you when you stand near an artillery piece, so impossibly loud that I didn't even hear the gun go off.

For a second I thought he'd tried to head-butt me, but his head had been driven forward by the explosion of brain, blood and skull from the rear.

It's an odd phenomenon. If you shoot a pumpkin off a fencepost it falls *toward* you because of the propulsion of matter exiting the big hole in the back. Shoot a man in the head and the same thing happens.

The entry wound, square in the middle of Hollis Carpenter's forehead, was smaller than a dime and neatly rimmed by glowing embers of burning powder and flesh. But the back of his head, for all intents and purposes, was now somewhere – everywhere – inside his front parlor.

The light left his eyes a heartbeat before the scene was frozen in an explosive flash of pure white as lighting leaped into a live oak not more than fifty feet away.

Hollis Carpenter toppled forward the same moment the tree fell backward, and thus began a week of fury wrought by vengeful men, raging nature, and the nightmare world that evolves when the two forces combine to strip way the fragile veneer of civilization.

Chapter 2

Tom Carmody, my deputy, rode back to the Carpenter place with me. I needed to pick up the body and then figure out what to do with it. Our local undertaker died and we never could find a replacement. So it's up to the marshal to find a claimant for dead bodies or to bury the bodies himself.

As of late, I'd been responsible for producing the bulk of the supply, so I suppose that's only fair.

Carpenter was a fairly big man, about my size, a little over six feet and maybe one-ninety. I probably could have hoisted him up by myself and slung him across a horse – I'd done as much with wounded men on the battlefield – but lifting a lifeless body is harder than most people think.

Besides, Carmody is freakishly strong and I hate to waste talent. So when I got back to town we borrowed a sorry little wagon pulled by two sorry and surly little horses and immediately headed back to Carpenter's place.

The horses didn't like the stinging rain any more than I did. I don't know if horses can actually feel resentment, but these two eyed me with such somber horse-faced reproach that I almost apologized out loud as I hitched them up.

Carmody, who is constructed primarily out of leather and scrap iron, doesn't much notice rain or cold or heat or any sort of discomfort, for that matter. Especially when his attention is diverted to the task of lecturing me.

"You let him get the drop on you," he said. His Eastern Tennessee twang thickens a bit when he's carried away with his moments of high drama. It came out: *Ye lettim git the drop on ye.*

He made a clucking noise with his tongue. Three times. He always does it three times, at precise intervals. Like a precision-engineered scolding machine.

"And you being an officer and famous fighting man and all," he lamented.

I knew what was coming next. He shook his head from side to side. Twice. More slowly the second time, portraying an infinite, long-suffering weariness.

Now, in case you're wondering, part of what he said was true, and part of it's not, so let me set the record straight.

First, yes, I'd let Carpenter get the drop on me. I'd known Carpenter to be a hothead and career lowlife, but I got caught up in congratulating myself on what a nice helpful man I was. As a result, I stood there smiling, right in front of his door, like I was an old lady dropping off a basket of chicken for the church social. When I'm thinking straight I always approach a door by keeping my hand on my revolver and standing to the side, keeping wood between me and anyone of whom I am slightly suspicious until I can see his hands and who's behind him.

As to the rest of the information I want to put on the record: My name is Josiah Hawke, and I'm the town marshal in Shadow Valley, Texas. I came here a couple years ago on the invitation of Elmira, whose place was being put out of business by goons who, among other acts of goonery, killed the previous marshal, Billy Gannon. Billy was the captain my unit, and like a lot of us who'd picked up the appropriate skills of warfare, he found employment in gunwork, generally but not always on the right side of the law.

Billy had left word with Elmira to wire me if something happened to him, and something did, and it involved four bullets in the side of his head.

It would have taken a very dangerous and tough man to kill Captain Gannon.

I found him. His name was Purcell and he *was* dangerous and tough and it wasn't easy to kill him but I did.

It turned out that Purcell was only hired help for a criminal enterprise as hardy as a family of cockroaches, and I've been busy stomping on them ever since. But that's a story for another time.

As to the war. Carmody was a sergeant. I was a lieutenant, an injustice for which he will never forgive me. We didn't know each other during the war and as far as I know we never crossed paths. Carmody, who grew up eating squirrels in mountains so remote even non-native squirrels shunned the place, served mainly as a Union scout in the Appalachians. The man can read terrain the way anyone else reads a newspaper.

While I was technically an officer, I wasn't the type with schooling in the niceties of formations and grand strategy and protocol for drilling troops. I was part of a unit that carried out "special tactical operations," which is what I liked to call them.

The people we inflicted them on called them dirty tricks. I guess in a way we were both right; it's a matter of perspective.

Carmody, who had been saving his exasperated sigh for the right dramatic moment, delivered it with appropriate pathos, and snapped the reins to spur the reluctant horses.

The wind had abruptly shifted and the rain was driving directly into our faces in a nasty, alive, aggressive way, like angry swarming insects turning on us. Carmody surreptitiously tugged down the brim of his bowler and gathered together the collar of the oiled leather pommel slicker he favored. For him, the tacit admission that the rain stung his eyes enough to make him lower the brim of his hat was equivalent to a lesser man breaking into tears.

I didn't have much sympathy for him. The brim of his rakish bowler was no more than an inch wide, so rain in his eyes was the price of vanity. When I hired Carmody – I'd found him languishing in the jail I'd inherited from Billy Gannon, and upon learning he'd personally beaten up a dozen of Purcell's men, *all at the same time,* I told him he could opt to finish his sentence or take up lawing on my side – he'd not been what you'd call a fashion plate.

In the intervening time he's supplemented his ten-dollar-a-week deputy's salary with the proceeds of exceptionally smart horse-trading and downright brilliant dealing at the Faro table and has thus evolved to vested suits and elegant English-style bowlers with narrow brims.

But somehow, on him, his fancy clothes still look like overalls and straw hats.

Personally, I favor a round, very wide-brimmed hat called the Boss of the Plains. It's not particularly stylish. In fact, it looks like something you'd wear while plowing a field, and has a conspicuous hole on the front and back, but it's high quality and I'm attached to it.

Elmira bought it for me and it cost her a lot of money. A few months ago I managed to lose it when it was shot off my head during an ambush. I know that sounds like a plot device out of one of those dime novels but it does happen. I've seen hats shot off men's heads many times in battle and have managed to have several of mine detached in that precise manner.

In any event, Elmira and Carmody went back to the scene a week later and retrieved it while I was home healing up from a shoulder wound. Carmody had told her that after I'd passed out from delirium

I'd kept him awake all night mumbling about losing my hat, and of all the people in the world, only Elmira would go to such lengths to locate something she knew I missed. And only Carmody could find a hat in a miles-wide swath of rugged terrain.

I jammed the hat down and tightened the collar of the rubber poncho that I'd both worn and slept on during the war.

The Boss of the Plains has a nice tight headband and is great for keeping out the sun and the rain, and the bullet holes don't leak much.

I leaned forward and was actually quite dry and comfortable until a bullet tore the damned hat off my head again.

Chapter 3

We heard the report of the rifle a split second later. The lag between the time the bullet hit my hat and when the sound reached us led me to believe that the gunman was about 200 yards away.

That was mostly guesswork, of course, as I didn't know anything about the load or bore of the weapon that was turned on us but it sounded like a big-bore slug when it buzzed past and the report was in a deep-throated bass typical of what we called buffalo guns. I'd had a major who had drilled us relentlessly in the particular skill of estimating the distance of gunfire based on the timing of the sounds, and while it's a great subject to talk about over a beer it's far from an exact science, especially in a hilly range where sound can bounce and echo.

But a good guess is better than no guess – which I admit is yet another guess on my part – so I drew my revolver and fired two rounds in what I ascertained was the general direction of the ambusher. I didn't have any expectation of coming close, but just wanted to give whoever had almost parted my hair something to think about.

Carmody and I grabbed our rifles and rolled off the left side of the wagon. I put my shoulder under the edge and heaved upward.

The wagon was heavier than it looked and I wasn't able to tip it on its side. Carmody caught on to what I was doing and pushed up with his left hand while firing his rifle one-handed with his right hand, which happened to be poised about a foot from my left ear.

The wagon settled on the sides of the wheels and the bed provided us a wall of sorts, maybe five feet tall by eight feet wide.

It rocked contentedly while we fired over the top.

Carmody was mumbling something.

Actually, he was shouting. I swiveled my head so I could use the ear that hadn't been concussed by that cannon he carried.

"I said," Carmody yelled, mouthing the words expressively, as though he were speaking to a dull-witted child, "that your dumb farmer hat is jinxed."

I didn't know what else to do but shrug.

"Like a fucking bullet *magnet*," he said.

About then I heard the buzz of rounds above our heads and twin claps of rifle fire punctuated by a hair's breadth between.

"Yep," Carmody said, following my thoughts. "Two shooters. That ain't no echo."

"Do you think the wagon bed will stop the bullets?

As if on cue, splinters of wood blew between us and a hole appeared, so wide that the rain blew through it.

"Nope," Carmody said.

"Then I'll draw their fire and flank them."

If Carmody said something after that I didn't hear it because I had to turn my throbbing left ear back to him as I sprinted for the nearest tree.

Chapter 4

The tree was about the diameter of my leg and wouldn't have provided cover for an underfed groundhog but it was a distraction. One of the things you learn when being shot at, assuming you survive – which, if you did, means that you actually learned something useful – is that anything that interrupts your assailant's line of sight can throw off his aim or cause him to miscalculate your movement. Maybe not by much and maybe not at all, but on the battlefield survival is an accumulation of small maybes.

I sprinted in a straight line to the tree. Theories differ, but it seems to me that if you're being shot at from the side there's no point in zig zagging because you're just moving toward and away from the same bullet path, and you're going to get hit whether you've zigged or zagged. It's all about speed; It takes an experienced marksman a couple seconds to draw a bead on a running target, and judging from the fact that they'd missed a few shots already I didn't think the ambushers were expert shots.

Several bullets, I perceived with the ear that Carmody hadn't deafened, buzzed behind me and I heard one slap into the dirt. I couldn't tell how far in back of me it hit and I wasn't about to stop and look, but for the time being I'd moved faster than they'd expected.

I'd actually moved faster than *I'd* expected. Being shot at is a terrific motivator. I reached the tree and stood sideways behind it for a split second, knowing Carmody would pick up the cue and provide me some cover.

I heard three shots from Carmody's buffalo gun and I lit out for some real protection, a stand of pines at the base of a hill.

As I ran, I fired my rifle one-handed in the general direction of the shots, trying to draw the attention of the gunmen as they turned their sights back on Carmody. I needed three seconds or so to make it to the stand, a long time being exposed, but I risked a look toward the ambushers anyway. Looking anywhere but where you're going subtly slows you down, maybe not by much but by enough that it might count seriously against you.

The wind had abated and the rain was pouring straight down, in sheets so thick I saw nothing.

And then I realized I saw everything I needed to see.

Chapter 5

We had them. If you do what Carmody and I do for long enough it becomes like a chess match. You know it's over four or five moves before the end because of the inevitability of your closing moves and your opponent's inescapable lack of alternatives.

They were halfway up a hill with about a twenty-degree slope and were crouched about ten feet apart behind the thick trunk of a fallen tree. The vertical rain had tamped down the smoke from their weapons and it hung above them in two cottony, three-dimensional billows. For all intents and purposes, there may as well have been a sign proclaiming, "ambushers hiding here."

I didn't even bother running the rest of the way to the stand. I stopped and put four rounds into the top of the log, two beneath each smoke-cloud. The log was probably four feet thick and a cannonball couldn't penetrate it at the center, but whoever was hiding behind it would certainly see and hear the splintering of the wood and unless their motive was suicide they'd keep a low profile until they figured out what to do next.

I ran to the stand and began working my way uphill, tree by tree. I needed time to reload my rifle but hadn't yet fired my sidearm or the five-shot Cooper I kept in my pocket so I was in no particular hurry, though I admit that I view a revolver primarily as something that's nice to have when your longgun isn't handy, so I wanted to assure that the rifle was at the ready.

Meanwhile, Carmody started his ascent. He crouched and ran a Z-pattern like a rabbit, exactly what you want to do when charging head-on.

For somebody six-five and probably 220 the man certainly could move. Even with his rabbit-run he'd covered half the distance in about five seconds, closing in on the twin clouds.

A head popped up from behind the log. I was looking through the rain and sparse pine branches but I could still see the eyes – as wide as half dollars, puzzled and uncomprehending, as they tracked Carmody charging them.

It was plain that the sight of a snarling gorilla who moved like a deer and wielded a rifle the size of the mast of a boat was the last thing our attackers expected. That was a good sign in itself. It betrayed their lack of experience.

In an ambush, charging the attacker is usually the best strategy because running away is exactly what the ambushers expect and are prepared for. And if there was convenient cover nearby they wouldn't have chosen that spot for an ambush in the first place.

The ambusher I could see panicked, dipped down, and then the vertical barrel of a rifle rose over the log. He brought his head up sort of sideways, in a tentative way, like he only wanted to expose one eye, and in a flash of realization and trepidation and uncertainty he remembered that there was another man somewhere to his left and he looked in my direction.

He saw me an instant before I shot him in the forehead.

Chapter 6

The dead man's compatriot was flanked, and he realized it, and then he panicked.

For a man in his position, there were two smart alternatives, neither of which he chose.

He could have thrown out his gun and surrendered. While there's no guarantee we wouldn't have killed him anyway, at least he stood a chance of surviving. As it happens, he would have. As a lawman, I'm not supposed to summarily dispatch people even if they do try to murder me. At least not before I find out why they tried.

Alternatively, he could have backpedaled uphill and sideways into the woods behind him. A man with even an elementary grasp of tactics would realize that if there's an advancing enemy to the front and one to the side you retreat at a diagonal, putting maximum distance between you and both attackers as quickly as possible and moving sideways to their respective lines of fire. It's possible he might have escaped, for a while, anyway, until we tracked him down.

But one of the cruel ironies of life is that if you don't know much, you don't know what you don't know. Even as we closed in on him, the second shooter didn't realize that he was playing our game and he wasn't really equipped to ante up at the same table.

Despite his murderous nature, he was an amateur at the process.

He never stopped to think that the rain and humidity would tamp down the smoke and give away his position, and he was clearly too dense to deduce that two men who'd immediately divided his field of fire and alternately covered each other while flanking him knew too much to succumb to his next moronic move.

Which was to stand bolt upright and attempt to fire at the man advancing in front and then, I assume, pivot and fire at the man to the left.

Maybe he was envisioning the stories he'd tell at the bar or the campfire about his eagle-eyed aim, how he stood tall as the bullets whizzed by him. Maybe he'd heard stories like that and believed them and believed he could do the same.

In any event, he never got the stock of the gun to his shoulder before we cut him down.

Chapter 7

Setting the wagon back on its wheels wasn't hard. After I retrieved my soaked and newly re-ventilated hat, I rocked the rig a few times and it tipped back. The horses were in a state of shock; they had abandoned their reproachful glare and now their pool-ball eyes bugged out at me with pure bewilderment.

They didn't know it but it could have been a lot worse for them. Their traces were long enough so they weren't twisted to the ground when the wagon was tipped over, and most importantly, they hadn't been shot. An ambusher who knew what he was doing would have shot the horses immediately in order to immobilize the wagon and eliminate the possibility of Carmody and I seeking momentary cover behind a standing horse.

The rain had tapered off but the trail was muddy and I couldn't maneuver any closer to the hill without getting stuck. I got as close as I could. If Carmody could find their horses – which seemed likely, because it didn't seem reasonable that the ambushers had walked a long way to find a position in the middle of nowhere – we'd hoist the bodies on their mounts and hitch the horses to the wagon.

And we still had to pick up Hollis Carpenter's body.

I heard the horses coming down just as I began retracing the same route I'd taken up the hill. When they emerged from the stand of pines, I saw that Carmody was riding the smaller horse, and he'd lashed both of the ambushers' bodies onto the second. It was slow going. As a rule, horses don't like going downhill, but Carmody knew how to nudge them along and help them pick their footfalls.

I was tempted to let on that I was amazed that a mere mortal could round up two horses and heave two full-grown men up top in the same amount of time it took me to right the wagon and dry off my hat, but I'd seen Carmody accomplish quite a few things out of the ordinary and I was alive today because of his particular abilities.

So I let it pass.

"What do you want to do now?" he asked, casually, as though we'd just finished lunch and were deciding whether to whittle or play horseshoes.

"That looks like a pretty good horse," I said, and Carmody nodded.

"We have to pick up Carpenter's body at some point," I said. "I know we're taking a chance, but I don't see any point in turning around now and coming back because I think we're less than a mile away."

Carmody nodded.

"So I'll ride ahead," he said, "and scout the trail to see if anybody else has a mind to kill us.

We'll load these bodies on the wagon now. Then you drive the wagon to Carpenter's and pick up his body. We'll hitch the other horse to the wagon and if there's trouble and you need to maneuver and you do your best to get on the free horse before you get your farmer hat shot off again."

I nodded. The sudden influx of dead bodies had complicated the logistics, but Carmody had it all figured out.

"Now, all that is based on several assumptions," Carmody said. "Number one being you ain't planning on killing nobody else, because if you is, maybe we should just go back now and fetch a bigger wagon."

I didn't want to encourage him so I just nodded as we unhitched the bodies from the horse and arranged them on the bed of the wagon.

"Or," he said, "maybe a wagon *train*. With a few spare horses. Mules, maybe; they can pull big loads even through soggy ground."

I shoved one body close to an edge of the bed and surveyed the amount of room left in the middle.

"We can comfortably fit one more corpse in the wagon," I said. "Appears we could accommodate somebody about six-five."

And I looked him up and down for a second.

Carmody put a foot in the stirrup swung a long leg over his saddle.

"Before I make my final mistake by riding our front and exposing my back to you," he said, "you got any thoughts on the obvious question? Why these two tried to kill us?"

"All I can think of is that somebody saw me shoot Carpenter, or heard about it, and figured I'd be back to get the body, and lay in wait to take revenge. They had a couple hours to plan."

"I never seen them before, either," Carmody said, skipping over some needless conversation. It reminded me why I liked working with him so much. He didn't ask me if I knew who they were, which I obviously would have mentioned if I had.

"Maybe they're relatives," I said. "Lot of Carpenters crawling about in these hills."

He shook his head.

"Maybe, but not with the same last name. The head-shot one's initials is B.I. The gut-shot is A.S."

"You found wallets?"

"Nope."

"Identification in the saddle bags?"

"Not there, neither."

There's no point in rushing Carmody when he's building up to a dramatic moment, so I just let it play out.

I didn't mind. We both needed a breather, the rain had stopped, and there was even a jagged reddish break in the clouds allowing a pale band of sunlight to sweep along the hillside.

He fished in his right-hand pocket.

"Found the initials on the back of these," he said, as two brass pocket watches, identical to the one that sent Hollis Carpenter into the rage that sent him into his death, dangled from tangled chains, twisting and glinting in the sun.

Chapter 8

Carmody had set all three watches in a perfectly straight line on the table and studied them intently as he drank what might have been his third, fifth, or twentieth shot of the evening. He had a superhuman tolerance for liquor so it was difficult to estimate his progress.

He moved the thick brass candlestick closer to the middle watch and the reflection of the flame danced on the metal of the cases. I assume the watches were made of brass, too.

The candlesticks were Elmira's idea. She insisted that the bar needed to be cozied up, whatever that might mean, and last month she bought five of them.

I protested vigorously but in vain, which is pretty much the way our relationship works day-in and day-out. From my standpoint, putting ten-inch metal clubs on tables frequented by drunks – and then sticking a burning candle in each – was an invitation to disaster.

To my mind it made as much sense as handing out extra ammunition at the door.

I was playing the piano, an old but serviceable upright Elmira had placed against the wall, and

I was in a bad mood. No one had yet come to claim the bodies, and policy was that they would be kept wrapped in blankets in the jail for one day and then buried if no one spoke for them. I'd thought up that particular policy somewhere after my fourth whiskey; I figured that if I had to take care of the bodies, I could make up any damn policy I wanted.

"Keep playing that funeral music," Carmody said as he set his glass down directly in back of the middle watch, "and people is going to start slitting their wrists."

And of course I responded by playing more loudly and slowing down the tempo a bit. The increase in volume was serving a dual purpose: In addition to drowning Carmody out, and, I hoped, annoying him, it was thundering again and the rain was roaring against the roof so I had to play louder to be heard.

"Or maybe slit *your wrists*," Carmody said, turning all three watches over in sequence. "Just so you know the popular sentiment. In show business they call it 'reading the room.'"

He continued communing with the timepieces and in a minute cleared his throat.

"I'm guessing you can't play nothing much friskier anyway," he said, "since your hands is all swole up but banging off them thick skulls the other night."

He never missed anything.

"I'm fine," I lied.

"I don't want your head to get as swole up as your hands, but I do have to admit you are among the finest prizefighters I've ever met and among the finest piano players I've ever heard."

"Thank you," I said, and pounded a little harder on the keys, and it hurt. I suspected my middle knuckle on the right hand had been broken, and pain shot all the way to my elbow when I moved my hand the wrong way. And as far as I could tell, for the time being, there was no right way to move it.

"And as far as *piano-playing prizefighters*, you are alone on top of that particular and unique mountain. Same for *fighting piano-players*. Damn strange career path, though."

He was right about the career part.

I started out my profession as a college professor, teaching in a small academy near where I grew up in southern Illinois. I was from a farming family and was never particularly erudite but I was a fast study and picked up philosophy, languages, music, and the like pretty quickly. But things changed for me and a few million others in '61, and over the next four years or so I trained with some special units and picked up the equivalent of a master's degree in mayhem.

After the war, I returned to teaching and lasted exactly one month. A pug and strongman in a traveling show called me out in front of a group of students and friends, betting me long odds that I couldn't last two rounds with him.

I wasn't particularly bothered by his goading but the possibility of impending violence, well, somehow got my blood circulating again. I'm not saying I *enjoyed* the war – no one with even near-normal sanity could ever say that after seeing what I saw. But it was like a part of me woke up from hibernation when I took him up on it.

He never expected me to beat him to death.

I never expected to kill him, either, but as I'd spent several years learning to fight with guns, fists, knives, rocks, or basically anything that could somehow inflict injury, he wasn't much of a challenge despite his bulk.

The pug took exception to me knocking him down at will and tried to gouge my eye out and I took *strong* exception to that and put some real steam in the next combination and he was dead before he hit the ground.

Prizefighting was technically illegal in that county but everybody always looked the other way until, I discovered, somebody wound up dead, and then the locals got pretty damned excited. I got out a few steps ahead of the local law and found it easier and more profitable to ply my new trade than my old one, and after a few years I'd put together a respectable record on various bareknuckle circuits.

But prizefighting is a young man's game, and as I entered my 40s I gravitated toward gunwork, generally on the right side of the law and more often than not behind a badge, and that – along with the murder of Billy Gannon – is what led me to my present employment as town marshal in this odd little half-heaven-half-hell I call home.

I flexed my aching fingers and started a new number. Carmody continued to glare at the array of watches, as though waiting for them to confess something to him.

He wiped his mouth carefully with the back of his hand, keeping the watches fixed in his gaze in a predatory manner, like he expected them to bolt and wanted to be poised to chase after them.

As was his routine, he'd given up on the repetitious and comparatively inefficient practice of pouring himself shots and started drinking directly from the bottle, from time to time offering me a pull which I politely declined, suspecting that he may have recently indulged in his favorite delicacy, an acquired taste from his mountain roots, *squirrel.*

As I fought back a wave of queasiness at the thought of what those lips might have recently feasted upon, he held up the empty bottle and called for Nonie to bring him another.

Nonie was about ten or eleven, we guessed, and she'd ridden into town a couple months ago in some sort of a trance after, we later learned, her family had been slaughtered by a marauding cult. It was the same bunch who later tried to kill me and Carmody.

Nonie can't talk. We figure what happened blasted her into some sort of state of shock and she lost her power of speech. She understands well enough, and Elmira put her to work around the

Spoon, fetching things and cleaning up, figuring it was best to keep her busy.

I christened her Nonie.

Elmira had been calling her "no-name," which I thought was a little impersonal.

Nonie never made a sound, ever – not when she burned her hand on the stove a month ago, and not even during last week's brawl, where she'd been tossed atop a moving mass of writhing piles of fighting men, wielding fists and, of course, those fucking brass candlesticks, and she was buffeted across the room like she was riding an ocean wave.

So it came as quite a surprise to me when she came over to Carmody's table, stiffened when she looked at the table, seized the middle watch, and screamed.

Chapter 9

Nonie's scream triggered a cascade of silence in the bar. I stopped pounding on the piano, which I had been hammering to drown out Carmody, and when Carmody heard how loudly his words rang out without musical accompaniment he stopped talking, and everybody at the bar reflexively ceased their conversations and looked over.

All we heard was thunder, rolling rhythmically after periodic flashes that lit up the windows.

She couldn't scream very loudly. I guess she was out of practice. After a few wails she lost her momentum and sounded like a cat meowing.

I picked her up and sat back down, depositing her on my lap, but I couldn't get her to stop.

Carmody stood up and reached out and said, "now, now, now, now, now" but apparently couldn't come up with a conclusion to the sentence, and frankly the sight of him towering above us with that wiry beard moving like a machine, outlined in the flashes of lightning, all the time saying "now-now-now," with that absurdly long arm outstretched, was starting to scare *me*.

Nonie covered her eyes and kept mewling.

Elmira bustled over and said, "stop screaming."

And she did.

"I didn't think a that," Carmody said.

"Me neither," I admitted.

Elmira plucked her off my lap and cut me a sideways glance with those eyes that I always characterized as clear and blue as a mountain lake. Now, they looked more like a frozen-over mountain lake. Or a glacier. I'd never seen a glacier, but I would surmise that's how they appeared.

"You scared her with that creepy funeral music," Elmira said.

I held my hands up the way you do to show you're not armed.

"It wasn't funeral music."

"It was cowpoked-up Chopin," Carmody said, invoking his term for my technique of adapting whatever stuff I could remember when I ran out of popular songs and war ditties. You can play anything on a tinny piano and give it a strong beat and it sounds like saloon music.

"And technically speaking," Carmody said, thrusting that finger-that-was-as-long-as-a-tree-branch in the air, "it *was* funeral music. Chopin's A minor Prélude."

And then he noticed the frosty glare that Elmira and Nonie lad leveled on him in unison. Nonie had picked up Elmira's mannerisms. Elmira held Nonie on her left hip and planted her fist on her right hip. Nonie mirrored the posture with her left fist on her left hip. They both levelled the identical icy glare.

"Chopin had it played at his own damn funeral," Carmody explained, as though anyone cared.

"How the hell do you know this stuff?"

I had to ask.

"I ain't no dummy," Carmody said, and took a pull from the bottle Nonie had brought him.

"Elmira," I said, "it had nothing to do with the music. She saw the watches we took off the dead men."

"The men you *killed*," she corrected.

"Yes, the men I killed."

"Today."

"Today."

"Today *so far*," she added.

I had no idea what was eating her at the moment but didn't see any point in providing the crowd any more saloon-theater, so I let it pass.

"To be fair," Carmody said, never one to miss an opportunity to pour kerosene on some glowing embers, "Josiah was *ambushed*. *Twice*. He didn't go out looking to kill nobody. And besides, I'm the one what killed the second man on the hill. Josiah here just pumped in a couple rounds after the fact so he could feel useful."

Elmira took a deep breath, always a bad omen of things to come, so I jumped in.

"Look," I whispered, although it was unlikely that anyone in the bar really couldn't hear me, "right now the important thing is finding out what's going on with Nonie."

I could feel the heat burning inside, heat that had bubbled throughout the day as various persons and persons unknown tried to kill me in a driving rainstorm, a heat that grew to a boil when I actually had to turn my boots over and pour water out of them when I got home, and a heat that threatened to drive steam out my ears at any second, and I gave Elmira a look that I hoped would convey in no un-certain terms that I didn't want to pursue the topic at hand.

I guess I overdid it – an important part of my business is scaring people, and I've gotten good at it — because her hand went to her mouth and she took a step back.

"What's the matter?" she said.

I sat down at the piano and played something cheerful, a quick and lively Stephen Foster song popular among the Union troops.

The crowd began turning back to whatever had occupied them a minute ago, burbling, almost instantly, as though I'd turned on a spigot.

"Josiah," Elmira said, softly, in the tone that you'd use to say, "no sudden movement" if you spotted a nearby snake, "I'm sorry. I know you didn't go looking to kill those men. It's just that af-ter that big fight here, and months and *months* of trouble, day in and day out, I'm just tired of it."

I kept playing. It hurt but it did loosen up my bruised knuckles. I wanted to remind Elmira that the reason I came here in the first place was to kill the men who'd killed Gannon and threatened her and her daughter.

I picked up the tempo as my fingers limbered up.

I also wanted to make it clear to her that I didn't enjoy laying the barrel of my gun alongside the heads of troublemakers who tried to bust up her bar. But that wouldn't have been entirely true.

So I didn't say anything.

"Josiah," Elmira said, "please, I'm asking again, *what's the matter?*"

I didn't want to continue the conversation, so I played a little louder.

Carmody had hoisted Nonie on his lap and was bouncing her on his knee in tempo with the camp song and I figured pretty soon he'd find it necessary to sing along, and I was right.

He possessed a clear and powerful tenor.

We live in hard and stirring times,
Too sad for mirth, too rough for rhymes;
For songs of peace have lost their chimes,
And THAT'S what's the matter!

Chapter 10

I waited about twenty minutes before I talked to Nonie. The crowd noise had picked up, so the piano wouldn't be missed, but things hadn't yet gotten raucous enough for me to feel the need to glare at anybody.

She was still on Carmody's knee. Elmira hovered in back of Carmody.

"Nonie," I said, "Tom wants to ask you some questions."

Elmira shot me a confused look but Carmody didn't miss a beat. One thing both of us knew, and the thing that has most improbably kept us both alive in recent months, is that we let whoever's best for the task at hand pursue it. I'm a better strategist. Although he may tell you different, I'm a better fighter. He's a better long-distance shot. He's a much better woodsman.

And when it comes to blarney, he's the undisputed world champion.

Tom Carmody could talk a dog off a meat wagon.

"Nonie, I don't like to talk much myself," he lied, "especially when I'm with people what I don't know I can trust. I know you been keeping to yourself since something horrible happened to you, and you're still making up your mind about Elmira and me and the marshal."

She looked directly into his eyes. I'd not seen her make extended eye contact before.

"You was surprised by seeing them watches," he said.

I noticed that she still held the watch clutched in her fist. Her knuckles were white and her hand trembled slightly, whether from emotion or exertion I could not tell.

"Right now we got a big mystery on our hands because them watches all came off people who for some reason tried to hurt the marshal and me. Now, we're pretty tough, but seeing as how we don't know why these guys is acting loco we need to figure out what's going on before somebody else gets hurt."

She nodded.

"You can help by telling us why you was so shocked when you seen them."

Nonie's eyes shifted focus to a point far away, and then she shut down.

"It's OK you don't want to talk," Carmody said. "But you can nod. You don't have to give away no secrets. You don't even have to say nothing if you don't want. You just nod if I say something and what I say is true."

Carmody didn't give her time to think about the deal.

"You went right for that watch in the middle when they was all face down. Didn't even look at the others. It was them *initials* on the back caught your eye. You seen that particular watch before, the one with the 'HC' on the back."

It might have been a nod. A small jerk of the head.

Carmody didn't pause.

"Thank you, honey." It came out, *thank-ye, hawnee.*

"I'm guessing that they guy who had that watch was involved in something bad," Carmody said. "He tried to hurt the marshal this morning and I'm guessing at one point he tried to hurt you or you saw him try to hurt somebody else."

She stiffened and started to get that faraway look again and Carmody cut in immediately.

"You don't have to answer. We already knowed he's a bad man, pretty clear he done something real bad, and all we want to find out is what him and these others was up to so's we can keep anybody else from being hurt."

Nobody said anything for a long minute and I was going to break the silence when Carmody held out his palm to me, out of Nonie's view.

Carmody was calm but I could tell that behind his level gaze there were gears turning and pistons firing. Behind that wiry beard and lips that feasted on corn liquor and squirrel there was a mouth directly connected to a brain that somehow categorized every piece of music known to mankind, remembered poems and scraps of literature word-for-word, and somehow could uncover a prized nugget of information like a prospector washing away the silt while panning for gold.

And when Carmody spoke next, I was struck as wordless as Nonie.

Chapter 11

"You done a real good job helping us clean up after that big fight here the other night," Carmody said, leaning in close to Nonie, their foreheads almost touching. "And I couldn't help but notice you was looking through everything, all the broke glass, the dishes, the pieces a chairs, like you was looking for something."

Her eyes widened and Carmody smiled and shook his head.

"It don't matter. But now I figure you was looking for that watch. You had it in one of your pockets and lost it when you was tossed about like a cork when all them guys was busting up the place. Me and the marshal felt real angry about them taking a chance on hurting a little girl like that, which is why I tried to peacefully restore order and the marshal here went crazy and cracked heads like they was eggs and he was making omelets for fifty cowhands on a trail drive."

Nonie smiled.

Elmira frowned. At me.

I frowned back and she looked away.

"You had that watch with you the day you rode into town, didn't you?" Carmody said. "We never went through your pockets or nothing before we put you in the bedroom Elmira set you up in once the girl and the customer cleared out."

Elmira cleared her throat and held a finger to her lips.

Carmody realized his error and got back on track.

"We went through the saddlebags on the horse and didn't find nothing. Never occurred to me or the marshal to search *you*. We should have. Not because you done anything wrong but because we might have found something that helped us figure out what happened when you and your family and that whole town was massacred."

Elmira started to speak but I caught her eye and shook my head.

Carmody's words were hard but not cruel.

Sometimes things have to be said.

"It was a rough time for sure," Carmody said, "and one of the men involved in hurting people in the town was a tall man with yellow teeth and in the midst of the fighting he dropped this watch and you picked it up when you ran away and kept it."

She gave an almost imperceptible nod.

"And you kept it because you knew that someday, somehow, you'd find a man with initials HC and make it so he couldn't hurt nobody again. Am I right?"

She gave an almost imperceptible nod. And then another. A decisive one.

Carmody held her by the shoulders, his absurdly large hands almost encircling her.

"I think that man is dead, and we have his body in the jail. I know it ain't right to ask a little girl to look at a dead body, but that's what I'm asking you to do. I need to know if he was part of that awfulness so me and the marshal can figure out *why*."

Carmody tilted his head forward.

"Will you do that for me, Nonie?"

She slid off his lap, stood ramrod straight, and – with the same look of resigned determination I'd seen a decade ago on the faces of kids sometimes only six or seven years older than Nonie, kids who grimly reconciled themselves into marching to war – she nodded.

Chapter 12

The rain cleared the next morning but Carmody's mood did not.

We sat in the back room of the Spoon. Bars don't smell great at any hour, but the fragrance of yesterday's beer, puke, and sweat packs a real punch at 9 a.m.

"I seen this weather before," he said, slurping coffee I'd inexpertly made a few minutes ago and scowling into the cup after each swallow. I'd warned him not get his hopes up.

"Storms that blow in from Mexico or Louisiana. They're different down here, different from what we're used to back east. They come in waves. Rain like hell for a while, dry up, and rain like a fresh hell the day after. These things can play out for days or weeks."

"You think it's going to be bad?"

He nodded.

"I can smell electricity in the air," he said. "The birds is acting funny. And the sky's got a strange red color. Red skies have been scaring the shit out of people back to Biblical days."

Carmody was a lay preacher during the war and while he'd grown cool on religion, he could quote chapter and verse on demand.

"In Matthew," he said, his voice slipping into his preacher cadence, "Jesus Christ looked up and said, 'It will be stormy today, for the sky is red and threatening.'"

He swirled the coffee and peered in the cup as though he expected to find something dead at the bottom.

"And what else is bothering you?" I said.

"For one thing, this coffee tastes like it's already been through a set of kidneys."

"Sorry."

"And not *human* kidneys, neither."

"Sorry."

Carmody set the cup down with more force than necessary.

"And just to make me even edgier," he said, "I don't know where to go with this Carpenter thing. We got random people trying to kill us and the only person what knows anything is a little blond-headed human clam."

Last night Nonie had nodded her recognition when we showed her Hollis Carpenter's body. She didn't know the other two.

And then she'd crawled back in her shell and closed the lid behind her.

"So we're nowhere," Carmody said.

"Not exactly, Tom. We know that Carpenter was somehow involved in that massacre. We know that Carpenter was linked to the ambushers for a reason that must be related to those watches. And we know that whatever that reason was it must have been serious, because when Carpenter saw me with the watch he assumed I was on to him and damn near shit himself before he pulled on me."

Carmody nodded but his thoughts were far away.

"By the way, hell of a piece of detective work getting the story out of Nonie," I said. "How'd you know where to go?"

"Lucky guesses, for starters. I knew she weren't going to come right out and tell me nothing and she keeps her face as still as a sphinx."

I nodded.

"Remember that guy I took for two hundred dollars last week?" Carmody asked, apropos of nothing. "Thought he was a real cool character with those cold, dead eyes and all."

"I remember."

"Well, every time he bluffed he'd swallow hard and his Adam's apple is about the size a my fist so I couldn't hardly miss it."

Carmody looked down at the empty coffee cup.

"I kept her on my lap and had my hands on her the whole time. Every time I got close to the truth she'd stiffen up."

"I know what you're thinking," I said. "You know you did the right thing but you feel bad about playing her like that."

"That's part of it, and you're right. The closer we get to finding out exactly what happened to her the better the chance we can help her."

"What's the other part?"

"It ain't necessarily a bad thing, but I cannot help but notice that I am turning into *you*. You remember what you said when we first teamed up? You said you was a genius reading people and I was a good partner because I was a genius reading tracks?"

"I never called myself a genius," I said, although I would not necessarily disagree with the assessment.

"Well, damn it," Carmody said, with unanticipated heat, "something about this arrangement just sticks in my craw."

I hadn't expected this, and I could feel a flash-fire of quick anger kindle inside me.

"What sticks in your craw?" I asked, keeping my voice low and even.

He fixed me with an intent stare for a full ten seconds, and then drew in a deep breath.

"In two years I've managed to pick up all your sneaky ways of finding things out," he said.

"But do you bother to learn anything from *me?*" Carmody asked. "You still can't find your own ass with both hands and a compass. What an *insult.*"

He was actually having trouble catching his breath between bouts of braying laughter, so I slammed the door as I left on my morning rounds, leaving him alone, hoping he'd somehow suffocate.

As I walked down the muddy street, my boots sucking in the mud, I could hear him slapping his knee and coughing.

Chapter 13

The problem with getting a laughing fit is that it becomes most uncontrollable at times when it's most inappropriate.

I was no more than five minutes into my rounds, up on the north end past the bank, when Hollis Carpenter's father rode out of the wooded trail, flanked by three goons and a riderless horse tethered to one of the mounts.

I heard them coming, of course, and knew that I would be in bad spot being on foot should they have hostile intent, but running back to the center of town would be bad for my image should anyone crawl out of bed and see me.

So I waited, watching them ride up, and there I was, a full-grown marshal with a glare that can paralyze my girlfriend, confronting the father of a man I'd killed and three thugs who likely wanted to mutilate me. And the first sound out of my mouth was a suppressed laugh that sounded like a pig snort.

I made a mental note that when I got around to killing Carmody I would do it methodically, imaginatively, and above all, slowly. I was still peeved at him for suckering me, but at the same time I had to admit he'd played the joke out pretty well.

"Mr. Carpenter," I said, and I coughed into my sleeve, trying not to laugh again.

Carpenter, genuinely puzzled, looked to the man to his left and then at the two to his right. All of them shrugged.

I normally don't carry a handkerchief but I'd stuck one in my pocket yesterday after using it to wipe the rain off my revolver so I pulled it out and coughed into it with convincing sincerity, I believe. I cleared my throat, determined that if I were going to be murdered I was not going to be giggling like a little girl when I drew my last breath, and tried again.

"Mr. Carpenter, let me get right to the point. I killed your son yesterday, and I surmise you're here to claim the body. I'm sorry about what happened, but I had no choice in the matter. He drew on me without provocation. I wrestled his gun away but it went off in the struggle."

"That ain't what I heard," Old Man Carpenter said. It occurred to me that I didn't know his first name. I'm not sure anyone in town did.

"What did you hear?"

Carpenter looked down at me and his nostrils widened, like he smelled something bad.

He was a completely gray man. Gray hair, gray beard, gray shirt and vest, and gray eyes that beamed a cold, gray hatred. I would take him to be in his mid-60s, but his gray aura was a glow of hard flint and cold steel, not of age.

He was a criminal of some note through a wide swath of Texas, exerting influence, I'm told, from Hill Country west almost to El Paso – which, if you're not familiar with Texas geography, is more than 500 miles, about the same distance as Chicago to the border of Tennessee.

"The boy of one of my hands was riding down from the hills," Carpenter said, "and was behind the pines and he saw you kill Hollis in cold blood. You didn't see him but he saw you. He followed you back to town and back out to Hollis's place when you took the body. The boy who saw you ain't more than twelve and couldn't do nothing but follow you all day. But he told me what happened."

I believed part of what he said. Hollis Carpenter's place was at the foot of two steep hills riddled with trails and the door faced most of one hillside. Somebody must have seen me in order for the ambush to be put in place, and a kid on a trail is as likely as any other option.

The rest, of course, was bullshit. While it's conceivable that a stealthy rider could have trailed me back to town, Carmody would have inevitably spotted a tail when we went back for the body.

No, the kid had notified somebody immediately, maybe Old Man Carpenter himself, and my guess is that they might have entertained the same worries as Hollis: that I'd figured out whatever the hell they were up to.

It didn't take a master strategist to figure out that a peace officer couldn't leave a body to rot and that I'd be back with a couple hours, probably with a wagon, and thus present an easy target.

Carpenter cleared his throat and injected just a little too much innocence into his question.

"What was you at Hollis's house for?"

I wasn't about to tell him the truth. I don't know if the witness would have been close enough to see all of what happened. If he had seen the whole business, Carpenter might not be so curious.

"To serve a civil warrant, that's all. Unpaid court costs from a theft case he was involved in a couple years ago. Didn't amount to more than twenty dollars. No reason for him to go berserk like he did."

After a few seconds of silence, Carpenter leaned forward and spat at my feet. The sound agitated his horse and it spun its head and took a couple of uneasy half-steps. Some mounts are skittish like that when they hear unexpected sounds, even soft ones, especially when they are not trained well. Some men who should know better regard their mounts as simply an interchangeable conveyance and never learn much about horsemanship, and sometimes don't outlive their animals as a result.

"You're a lying shit, and you're a cold-blooded killer. I'm going to take my son's body back for burial and when I'm done I expect to find you and that idiot deputy gone from this town. That badge don't give you license to murder. People round here are on to you. There's a shitstorm coming down on your head and you can't do a thing to stop it."

"Don't forget the other two bodies," I said, ignoring his threat.

"Don't know nothing about two other bodies," Carpenter said, too quickly.

Carpenter snapped the reins and rode forward.

I could tell immediately what he was up to. He wanted to veer toward me gradually as he pretended to begin to ride away, and when he pulled to the left, as I knew he would, the meaty shoulder on his mustang would send a thousand pounds of horse thudding into two hundred pounds of me.

I don't know if he wanted to knock me down to teach me who was boss, or whether he fully intended to trample me to death. I had a feeling he didn't know either, and was just going to let improvisation take its course and claim the whole business was an accident.

Gunplay was not out of the question but I didn't think it would come to that, at least not now, not in the north end of town, even a town populated largely by drunks who were still comatose. Even in my particular ass end of civilization gunning down a marshal is likely to bring unwanted attention. Laying a beating on him, especially in the guise of an accident or provocation, just might draw a pass, especially if you're wealthy and connected.

Aside from that, even though there were four of them and one of me, the appearance of a gun would in almost any circumstance result in at least one of them being shot.

So this was going to start with assault by horse. I wondered if there's an actual crime by that name. I made a note to look it up.

Or write up an ordinance after the fact and use it to stick Old Man Carpenter in jail for a while.

Chapter 14

I was never formally in a cavalry unit, but did my share of riding alongside them, and cavalrymen often told a joke that held a lot of truth.

The question was, what spooks a horse?

The answer: Things that move, and things that don't.

By nature, horses are skittish animals, afraid of predators and not particularly well-equipped for self-defense. You can to an extent breed that out of an animal, and given the right horse, train it to be stoic and even heroic. The right horse, say, a big Morgan, could – after long and gradual exposure to gun and artillery fire – not only learn to ignore the sound but charge directly into it.

That type of training is tedious and expensive, which explains why a cavalry horse often cost more than a good-size house.

Carpenter's horse was clearly not trained, nor well cared-for. The hooves were not well-trimmed and I could see untreated bite-marks on its withers and crest.

That told me all I need to know about the horse and its rider.

So I screamed and clapped my hands and the horse reared.

Carpenter suddenly found himself leaning back at a 45 degree angle and tried to tighten up on the reins but I reached up and grabbed him by the back of the collar and pulled him straight backward, pulling down and then, when he landed, driving his head into the muddy road as hard as I could manage.

Chapter 15

Carpenter's men did what thugs do when their plans are disrupted.

The looked from one to another, hoping to see some intelligence flicker from behind someone else's eyes.

Sensing none, they reverted to type and grunted some meaningless threats.

"Get away from him," said the apparent leader, a beefy man with a coal-black beard and mean little eyes.

"So you can trample me? Why wait? Do it now."

Carpenter was flat on his face, unconscious for the moment but beginning to stir.

I put one foot on his back.

"Go ahead," I said. "Grind up your meal ticket."

A kid to his left, lanky with greasy hair and an eye that pointed oddly in a different angle from the other, edged his hand incrementally toward his sidearm.

"An inch closer to that gun," I said, "and I'll shoot out the eye you've got pointed in my direction."

He jerked his hand back as though the gun were hot.

A few months back I'd burnished my reputation by shooting the gun out of the hand of someone who drew on me. A local paper had written it up. Truth be told he'd gotten the drop on me and I squeezed off a panic shot that could have just as likely gone into the air or into my leg, but a bullet has to go somewhere and in this case it hit the tip of his gunbarrel.

I had seen no reason to ask for a retraction of the story as it occasionally does me some good.

I think they were scared to start a gunfight.

Maybe they read the papers.

They exchanged glances again and did not come to any consensus of strategic brilliance.

"You jumped Mr. Carpenter," Blackbeard said. "He wasn't doing *nothing* to you. All he wanted was to pick up his kid's goddamn body. You might a hurt him bad. He needs tending."

Blackbeard slid a leg over the saddle.

"We're taking him back. And then we're going to the law."

"I'm the law."

"We'll find some other law," Blackbeard said.

He dismounted and held his hands palm-out in the I'm-not-looking-for-trouble gesture, but kept them at shoulder height, which is also a convenient position for throwing a punch or drawing a gun.

And, of course, a squat man with a flat nose and a shovel-shaped face, who had edged his horse to my left and out of my line of sight was sliding down, thinking he'd sidle up in back of me. That's the way it usually works.

It was an interesting standoff. Everybody was standing in back of a line they didn't want to cross.

Most fights are like that, even on the battlefield. Most war is rarely all-out. You generally, for example, don't execute prisoners even though you might like to, out of hatred for past wrongs. You know full well they are a liability in terms of logistics and food supply and they may mount an attack against you or reappear on the battlefield after they've escaped or been traded. But there's something that usually holds you back from summarily killing them.

For some, putting limits on fighting is an ethical issue. For others, it's a matter of practicality. If I routinely kill the other side's prisoners, the reasoning goes, they'll kill their prisoners, which could include my comrades and possibly, someday, *me.*

The four creatures surrounding me were not, I surmised, much interested in the philosophy of human conduct, but they wanted to keep this from escalating into gunplay.

I'm not sure they had a fully thought-out plan when they came into town. But finding me alone and on foot in the deserted north end on a Sunday morning, they'd figured, under Carpenter's lead, to hurt me. Maybe even hurt me enough to kill me, but as a practical matter gunning me down in front of potential witnesses had some practical drawbacks, such as a potential visit to the gallows. Moreover, this wasn't like shooting me in the back during an ambush from high cover. I was in a position to shoot back, and they knew, probably from reading about my implausible marksmanship, that it was likely I could hit at least one of them. Hired help generally doesn't like those kinds of odds.

They wanted a scuffle, preferably one that could somehow be blamed on me, and wanted to hurt me enough that I'd run away and raise sheep or something, or at least keep my nose out of their business. Perhaps, in the best of all possible worlds, they could get me out of lawing altogether in the event I was trampled to death in a melee of my own making.

But Old Man Carpenter was my lucky charm. Because he paid the bills, they couldn't very well trample us both.

And time was growing short for them. As far as I could tell, no one in town had spotted us yet, but I didn't know that for sure and neither did they.

Sooner or later someone who actually gave a damn – a sliver of the local population, to be sure, but I'd made a few friends in the past year – would see what was happening and track down Carmody.

So they banked on having Blackbeard move toward me under the pretense of tending to Carpenter, and Shovelface grabbing me from the rear, or maybe scrambling my brainpan with the barrel of his gun.

I could hear Shovelface creeping toward me. I'm sure he felt he was moving as stealthily as a jungle cat but he sounded more like a three-legged mule.

Blackbeard was eight feet in front of me, give or take an inch. If you have a hundred or so professional fights you will definitely dull many of your faculties but your ability to judge distance will be as accurate as any surveyor's device.

I wasn't worried about Shovelface yet, who I sensed was still a good fifteen feet away and moving slowly and clumsily. If he wanted to shoot me, he could, but he could have just shot me from horseback, so I presumed that was not his plan.

Blackbeard still had his hands upraised but moved them a couple inches forward. His face was a study in angelic innocence.

So that's where I kicked him.

Chapter 16

A moderately tall man can cover a lot of ground with a kick.

I took a long step forward with my right leg, snapped forward with my left, and planted the ball of my left foot right on his mouth.

It's called a push-kick, and I'd learned that from a fighter who'd trained in Siam. It's not hard at all if you're limber and your pants aren't too tight. Most fighters don't expect a kick that high and aren't prepared to block it. If they do catch your leg, they have to tie up one or both hands to hold onto it, so if you can do some fancy hopping you can punch their unprotected face.

I had a hunch no follow-up would be necessary because Blackbeard stiffened and began to topple backward.

But I didn't stop to admire my work. That's the mark of an amateur, and the main reason why amateurs tend to get shellacked from behind. So I stepped back and pivoted; if Blackbeard were still conscious it would take him a couple seconds to either come after me or give into temptation and shoot me.

Shovelface was, as I suspected, closing in with his right fist drawn back. I think he'd planned on grabbing my shoulder, turning me around, and pasting me in the jaw, a tactic he may have seen employed in a bar-fight against a cooperative drunk.

He didn't expect me to turn nor did he anticipate that I'd slide right back to where I started. I was right on top of him.

Shovelface threw up his hands in a fighting stance, both hands protecting his face.

So I left-hooked him in the liver, aiming at the floating ribs and driving up toward the center of his back. He had a paunch, and I damn near buried my hand up to the wrist.

A liver punch hurts like no other, and it takes a second to register, but when it did he screamed and went down to a knee. I roundhouse kicked him, my shin cracking on his temple, and completed my revolution to keep the combatants in front of me.

Blackbeard was flat on his back making odd, fluttery noises with his lips.

Carpenter was awake, trying to lift his head and claw the mud from his eyes.

And Beanpole, the only man remaining on horseback, was drawing his gun.

Chapter 17

Normally I don't point guns at people unless I intend to shoot.

People tend not to take you seriously if you use a firearm as a gesture, and they also tend to kill you in the process.

But Beanpole's heart wasn't in it and he'd barely cleared the holster when my Colt was pointed at his forehead. He froze, uncertain of whether to turn his slow draw into a quick suicide by raising the barrel another inch.

"Jeffers, drop the gun."

It was Carpenter, groggy but alert enough to say Beanpole's name first so I didn't think he was telling me to drop my gun and lead me to think he was armed and hence shoot him.

Carpenter was up on his elbows and hadn't gone for his gun but I couldn't help but think that if he had, I very well could be ventilated by now. I promised to kick myself later for my inattention and fought off the urge to kick Carpenter now, just for the fun if it.

Beanpole Jeffers, clearly no master of the gun trade, *threw* the damn thing on the ground like it was on fire. Carpenter and I both flinched.

Luckily, the ground was damp enough that the revolver didn't hit hard enough to discharge.

I picked it up and stepped over Carpenter and took his sidearm. I kept everybody in my line of sight as I searched and disarmed the unconscious men. Neither had anything of immediate interest in their pockets.

I told Jeffers to dismount and raise his hands so I could search him for other weapons.

After patting him down, I drove a right to the point of his jaw and he was out before he fell. I didn't do it as revenge for pulling on me, although I didn't feel badly about it either, but I saw no point in trying to manage two men who'd already shown their intention to do me harm.

Besides, I had something in mind and wanted Carpenter to myself.

Chapter 18

It became apparent that Carpenter wasn't going to tell me anything.

I hauled him to his feet and shook him by the collar a little but he wasn't the least bit scared. He knew, or surmised, that I didn't make a habit of beating information out of people, at least not in these circumstances. While I generally don't believe in torture, I'd turned a blind eye to it a couple times during the war, when lives were at stake and time was short and a captured enemy held information about where people who were trying to kill us would strike next.

But that wasn't the case here. True, Carmody and I had been fired on, I think at Carpenter's behest, and I'd almost fallen victim to my soon-to-be-written crime of Assault by Horse, this time clearly at Carpenter's hands. But while there was some shady undercurrent of violence here, there was nothing imminent that I could detect.

From a practical standpoint, while Carpenter was a known criminal he was also a well-connected criminal, and if I brutalized or killed him I'd likely stir up a political shitstorm.

Moreover, I could tell from those cold gray eyes that I could beat on him all day and not get a thing out of him. Something in his demeanor told me he'd been through the process a few times before and didn't crack then, either. And while he was in his 60s, from the bit of roughing-up I did lay on him, I could tell he was still put together out of old iron and coiled springs.

So I settled for searching him, ostensibly for weapons, before I let him pick up his son's body, wake up his compatriots, and ride out.

I thought about asking Old Man Carpenter his first name, but I didn't want to get him thinking about why I'd asked.

So I settled for learning his first initial, which was R.

I saw it on the back of the watch, a timepiece identical to the three others, that I snatched from his pocket while looking for weapons and swiftly shoved back, demonstrating in convincing fashion, I hoped, my complete and utter lack of interest.

Chapter 19

Carmody literally stood before my desk hat-in-hand.

To be specific, he was clutching that silly bowler and standing, head bowed, as the rainwater dripped off him and puddled up on the office floor.

"I am deeply sorry," he said.

"Thank you," I said.

I waited and nothing was forthcoming.

"Is it anything *in particular* you're sorry about?"

He looked at me as though I were a slow child.

"About letting you get jumped by Carpenter and his men. I let you go off on your lonesome and didn't hear nothing 'cause I headed off in the other direction right after you left the office. I shoulda knowed to keep my nose in the air after we was ambushed like that."

"Oh, *that*," I said. "You had no way of knowing. I thought you were apologizing because you told me I couldn't find my ass with both hands and a compass."

He shook his head gravely.

"A course not. That was *funny*. I made you fall for that fair and square."

I thought about giving him a taste of my fearsome glare but thought better of it.

"I was missing in action," Carmody said, "because I went to the Widow Dwinn's."

"So you were a half-mile in the other direction. Even a bat couldn't hear a scuffle from that distance."

Carmody took a deep breath.

"I was satisfying my carnal desires."

"Jesus Christ," I said, but recovered in a second.

"What you do on your own time is your own business," I said, and fussed with some papers.

"I been helping her out on Sunday mornings," Carmody said. "A ranch like that, not easy for a woman, even one of her...her *dimensions*, to handle."

"Nope, not easy," I said, and pulled some more papers out of a drawer. As many papers as I could find.

"Look at all this shit," I said. "More circulars in the last month than the whole year before. Railroad robberies all over the place."

Carmody knew all about the robberies and, unmercifully, wasn't about to be distracted.

"Even a small ranch takes a huge amount of work," Carmody bulled on. "Hell, painting the fence is damn near a full-time job. By the time you get back to where you started it's time to start over again, and as...*capable* as she is, she just can't manage."

Dorothea Dwinn was over six feet tall and seemed to be constructed entirely of knees and elbows connected to a huge jaw. Her husband had died several years ago as a result of his drinking problem. His problem was that he'd gotten drunk and slapped her, and she'd caved in his head with a fireplace poker. That was the story I'd heard, anyway. It all happened before I'd come to Shadow Valley.

"Anyway, one thing kept leading to another, and lately I've –"

"Christ," I said, desperate to change the subject, and no longer feigning interest in the circulars I'd never actually bothered to read. "I had no idea. A train near Austin was robbed of a hundred thousand dollars' worth of gold. It was hidden in the floor and they still managed to find it. And this happened the night after a train was robbed of a cash shipment near San Antonio in the morning."

"She ain't at *all* like you'd expect, Josiah," Carmody said, having none of my diversionary tactic. "She don't really dress to suit her figure, but underneath all them sack cloths and old grain sacks..."

I interrupted again, this time as much out of genuine astonishment as self-preservation.

"So the Pinkertons and railroad police were lured down south in the morning, and some of the guard on the train up north was drawn away."

I shuffled through a couple more.

"A *lot* of these robberies. And sabotage to tracks and equipment. All looking like it's somehow coordinated."

Carmody cleared his throat.

"Anyway," he said, turning the hat in endless circles like it was a wheel, "that's all I have to say."

I set the circulars back in the pile of mail that I vowed I really should read in the future.

"You can't be expected to babysit me twenty-four hours a day," I said. "But I appreciate the thought."

To set the record straight, I did *not* appreciate the thought. I couldn't get the thought of Carmody and the Widow Dwinn out of my mind.

I decided I needed a drink.

Chapter 20

As I turned the corner, I saw that Elmira was standing on a chair outside the Silver Spoon trying to re-hang the sign on the brackets about eight feet high, to the left of the door. When she raised her arms holding the flat piece of wood the wind caught it and she toppled to the ground, landing heavily on her left side.

I ran over and helped her up.

Her hair blew straight back and with her determined and fierce expression I thought she looked like a lioness with a golden mane. She picked up the sign with her right hand and hitched up her skirt with the left.

"I'll do it," I said.

"That's all right. I'm already muddy."

I made a grab for the sign.

"Look, let me do it. I don't think I need the chair, and if I can't reach it I'll call Carmody..."

And then it hit me. She *was* muddy. *All over.* On her left side, her right side, and her back.

"Did you fall down before?" I asked.

"Yes," she said.

"Just now?"

She nodded in agreement.

"When you tried to put the sign up?"

"Yes," she said, puzzling at my question.

"How many times?"

"Three. Three times before just now."

"And each time when you lifted the sign up the wind took it and blew you off the chair."

Her expression clouded and she turned her head to the side and regarded me out of the corners of her eyes.

"Josiah," she said, "where are you going with this?"

"Nowhere," I admitted, and I instantly knew I was right.

Chapter 21

After Elmira had cleaned up and dried off she sat next to me on the piano bench while I played.

I tried my damnedest to avoid playing anything she might know out of fear that she might try to sing. She is *genuinely* tone-deaf. Most people who say they are tone-deaf aren't; the fact that they can perceive that they are off-pitch proves that they have some concept of pitch. Elmira had no such concept, nor any inhibitions. Given the opportunity, she will howl out wildlife sounds that hold no relationship whatsoever to the tune.

I distracted her by telling her about Carmody and the Widow Dwinn.

Elmira's eyes are unusual in that they are not only wide and clear-blue as a mountain lake, but when she's surprised you can see the whites all the way around the eyeballs.

I noted that she can also go for an extraordinary amount of time without blinking.

"The *Widow Dwinn?*" Elmira asked, for about the fifth time.

"I don't know much about her," I said. "I've only met her once or twice, and the killing of her husband happened long before I got here. Is it true that she killed her husband?"

"She chews *tobacco*," Elmira said, unblinking, as though in a trance.

"So does Carmody. Did she really kill him with a fireplace poker?"

"Everybody here has a story," Elmira said, and I nodded agreement.

Elmira's story began when she was kidnapped as a child by Apache raiders who'd killed her family. While it seems strange that Apaches would kill some in a family and raise others as part of *their* family, it happened more than you'd suspect and I've learned that you just drive yourself crazy trying to apply one culture's logic to another.

Elmira had a child by an Apache, a warrior who was later killed by a Comanche, and she escaped with her baby and took to working in the bordellos, the only option, she said, for someone of her means and background. She had a head for business and teamed up with her former husband, Bannister Adler, to open the Silver Spoon.

They'd done pretty well for themselves but Bannister had a taste for the girls and liked them young, and that predilection extended to Elmira's daughter Cassie, who tired of his attentions after several years and summarily knifed him to death.

And that's when I'd joined this odd little group. Billy Gannon had left word with Elmira to bring me in should he meet an untimely death, and one of the things I discovered was that Billy was killed by the same crowd who tried to drive Elmira out of business so they could force her to sell her property to them.

The scrubland in back of the bar just happened to sit along the path of a planned railroad and would therefore soon multiply in value a thousand-fold – a fact that only a connected few knew.

Elmira refused to sell, saying it was the only life she knew, and I'm sure there was some truth in that.

But the other reason was that Billy had hidden Bannister Adler's body somewhere in the brush without telling Elmira where. Billy stashed the body temporarily, I'm sure, but was killed before he could do a thorough job. Elmira, even though she searched frantically for days, couldn't find the body and was terrified that the new owners *would* – and the story about her daughter would come out.

I promised her I'd fix things and I did. Carmody found Bannister's body in an afternoon. I made Bannister's body and any history of the crime disappear, and I killed the gunman pulling the strings of the campaign against her.

Cassie had gone to live with Taza, an Apache who'd tried to kill me, and who I'd beaten up, and who then proceeded to save my life twice in the interim so he could someday kill me slowly, at his leisure.

And the planned railroad, we were told just a few months ago by someone who should know, had been re-routed.

So all that blood, as so often happens, was shed for nothing.

I finished up some cowpoked-up Mozart and leaned over and kissed her.

"You're right," I said. "Everbody's got a story."

Elmira looked at me as though what I said didn't register, which I'm sure it didn't.

"And she spits all over the place," she said.

Chapter 22

I woke up well before dawn to the sound of Carmody pounding on the door and yelling for me to *git yerself up*.

"Hate to bother you," he said when I cracked open the door, "but you better a look at what all is happening."

The first thing I noticed was that my head hurt.

Then I observed that the world was coming to an end.

The roar of the wind was like a freight train. I know that people use that expression casually, but it really did sound like a freight train, just as I imagine one running right over me would sound.

I went to the window but backed off when I saw the glass bowing inward. If the wind popped it the shards would explode a grenade, so I retreated.

"Can't believe you're sleeping through this," he said.

"I drank enough to sleep through surgery," I said, pulling on my pants and stomping into my boots.

"I don't know exactly what we can do, but we better be on duty."

"You're right," I said. "Let's set up a command post in the office."

"What about Elmira?"

I laughed in spite of myself. I'd been doing a lot of that lately. This time I think it was because I was still drunk.

"You haven't slept with her," I said.

"Course not." He held up his hands in an *I'm innocent* gesture.

"Sorry, I haven't come to yet and I'm not making sense. What I meant was that if it's before eleven in the morning, you might as well try to resurrect a corpse. She'll be all right here. In any event, here's as safe a place as any."

Carmody didn't believe me and shook her by the shoulder.

"Elmira, get up. There's a bad storm. You'd be better off downstairs."

Carmody shook her by both shoulders but her head just lolled and bounced.

"Is she all right?" he asked.

"I told you."

"Nobody normal is that dead to the world," Carmody said, lifting her to a sitting position.

"Elmira," he shouted. "Can you hear me?"

She flexed her lips a little as though using them for the first time.

"Carrots," she said.

We elected to move her and the bed as far as possible from the window – the *winder,* as Carmody called it – and covered her with as many blankets as we could find.

Chapter 23

We lit every lamp in the office to make our presence known to the townsfolk.

Come dawn we would make rounds as best we could. It wouldn't be easy; it was an effort leaning into the wind to make it to the office and we were both breathing hard when we made it in.

It was a dangerous wind. So far nothing structural had collapsed, owing less to quality construction than to the fact that towns like Shadow Valley tend not to build anything too high or ornate. A window at the pharmacy had blown in, but the owner, Vern Miller, lived about fifteen minutes away – under normal conditions – and a ride out there to notify him wasn't worth the risk. Maybe I could figure out a way to cover it with a piece of wood after dawn. Many signs were gone, including the Spoon's. I thought for a second about trying to locate Elmira's sign but then realized that for all I knew it could be in Austin by now.

Carmody made some coffee.

"I told you this was coming when I saw that blood-red sky," he said, pouring out of the battered tin pot into two equally mistreated tin cups.

"Yes, you did. What comes next?"

"Floods," he said, and took a careful sip.

I waited for him to continue. When he's giving one of his lectures, he likes to take his time regardless of the urgency of the circumstances.

"I believe we're on the tail end of a hurricane," he said. "Probably one that worked its way in from Galveston or Corpus Christi or sideways-like from New Orleans. Hurricanes is like waves in the ocean. You get strong parts, weak parts, and then strong parts again. Usually stronger until it passes."

"When will it pass?"

"I think the wind, soon. Real hurricanes don't usually come this far inland 'cause they die out over land. But that don't stop the rain and with the hills we get big torrents. If I had to guess, I'd say the bank is a goner."

The founders of Shadow Valley, whoever they may have been, although I feel it safe to assume they were not engineers, saw fit to build the bank on land bordering the delta of two streams. It flooded regularly, even in moderate rainfall. Last year I was instrumental in burning most of it down – a story for another time – and the owners balked at the cost of a new building and re-built on the same sodden spot.

"When will the floods come?"

Carmody fished out his watch, the one I'd bought for him after he coordinated a complex rescue that saved, among others, *me*, so I owed him. We'd borrowed it from a local jeweler because

Carmody needed to arrange a series of arrivals and departures.

It occurred to me that when this was over we needed to have a talk with that jeweler about the pocket watches we'd been harvesting off local thugs, but put the thought out of my head while we dealt with the issue at hand.

"It's 4:45 now," Carmody said, snapped the cover shut, and thought for a full minute, drumming his fingers on the desk.

I have no idea what goes on inside his head when he goes into those thinking spells. Maybe he was summoning up a mental map of the streams and tributaries uphill and upriver from us, or doing some estimations involving the amount of rainfall per hour, or maybe he just wanted to make me believe his prediction was the outcome of some sophisticated calculation so I would take it seriously.

"Eleven," he said.

Chapter 24

A wall of water cascaded into the bank at 11:01.

That's what the bank's clock said, and while time around here is sort of a collective hunch – the bank manager sets the clock by looking up at the sun at mid-day, and those who have watches and clocks set them according to his best guess – I was impressed with Carmody's predictive powers.

The bank manager, a nervous little man named Jasper Lovejoy, hadn't made it in until about 10:30. His house was cut off from town by a stream that had swollen to ten times normal size, and it took some fancy maneuvering for him to find a place where his horse could ford it.

Carmody and I kept swinging by the bank until Lovejoy rode in. We were on horseback. The water was beginning to rise in the streets and horses have quite a bit more ground clearance than we did, along with that extra pair of legs for stability in swift current.

Carmody has unusually acute eyesight and spotted Lovejoy coming over a crest.

"He's waving his hands and slapping himself in the head," Carmody said. Man's beside hisself. Looks like he's plumb out of his mind."

"Means the same thing," I said, having nothing better to do while we waited, or, at least, until Lovejoy got close enough that I could see Lovejoy's paroxysm. "'Beside' and 'outside' used to mean the same thing, and early English used it to mean 'out of his mind.'"

Carmody nodded and figured out a way to top me.

"Like the translation in the King James Bible: 'Paul, thou art beside thy self, much learning doeth make thee mad.'"

I knew there was more coming.

"It was in *Acts, 26:24.* Don't know if they taught you that when you was going to school to become a professor."

He said it *perfesser.*

"Too much learning making a man crazy," Carmody said. "Interesting concept. Reckon that's what mighta happened to you?"

Just then Lovejoy saw us and let out a series of panicky whoops. Like some sort of bird call.

"This man apparently done a *lot* of learning," Carmody said out of the corner of his mouth, "because he sure has gone loco."

Lovejoy had dark eyes and a pointy noise and coal-black hair swept back from a low forehead. He'd lost his hat, if he had worn one, in the wind, and his hair was matted sleekly to his skull. His eyes darted manically between us and the bank. And he kept making the whooping noise.

He sounded like a bird but looked like an insane mole.

"We need to do something," he said, and waved his arms and whooped. "We need to do something."

I told him that we expected a crush of water soon and that whatever couldn't fit in the safe or the small vault should be bundled up and moved to the jail. We figured the safe and vault were too heavy to be pushed anywhere even if the whole building were toppled, but anything else we'd lock in the cell for safekeeping.

Lovejoy shooed us away with a frantic gesture of panicky, flitting fingers.

"I'll bring it over, I'll bring it over."

"You can't. You can't," Carmody said.

I wondered if Carmody was making fun of him or if Lovejoy's mannerisms were contagious.

"You'll drown. You'll drown," I added.

Lovejoy dismounted, plucked a ring of keys from his coat, and waded to the front door. The water was already ankle-deep and swirling.

"Go away. Go *away*," he said, and stamped his foot like a toddler, splashing us.

Carmody spoke softly.

"I'm going to say this once. We got a crisis and can't fuck around here any longer. Lock up what you can, grab what you can grab, and we're all going to get out of here."

Carmody's quiet menace scared Lovejoy. It scared *me*, for that matter, and I'm the one with the glare that can mortify girlfriends.

We each carried a bag of undetermined contents – Lovejoy had stuffed various papers into various bags seemingly at random – after wedging almost all the loose cash into the safe.

He hooted the whole time and kept glancing longingly toward his office as Carmody and I implored him to leave.

Carmody finally grabbed him by the back of the collar, told him that if there was something else get it *now,* and when Lovejoy burst into tears Carmody pretty much lifted him off the ground and Lovejoy reluctantly danced a panicky tiptoe ballet step as we escorted him out.

The water was up to our knees and pushing with mighty insistence by the time we'd mounted up.

We rode away but kept the horses to a trot because we were unsure of the footing

There was a groan and cracks like rifle shots, and we looked back and saw the building start to break loose from its foundation.

Chapter 25

The wind began to die down at two, but the water kept rising.

And so did tempers.

Vern Miller, the druggist, had managed to make it in before noon on a forlorn little horse with a narrow face that somehow resembled Miller. They could have been relatives.

Miller was a man of sublime mystery. Even his appearance gave few clues: He was a spare, sour fellow probably about 70, give or take twenty years in either direction. He wouldn't talk much about his past, although I'd had two interactions with him that led me to believe he'd seen more combat than the aggregate total of most infantry divisions. When I first met him he'd used a musket, of all things, to drill a bank robber who was sighting in on me. I had a hunch the thing had been hanging over his fireplace since the Mexican War and when the time came he plucked it down and used it exactly once, which is all you need if you know what you're doing, and he did.

The second incident involved him grafting himself onto a rescue party headed by my old commanding officer, Major Munro, who is now a state senator.

Carmody and I had both tried to get Miller to turn around and go home, fearing not only for him but for ourselves if we had to divert our attention to look after him, but Munro had recognized something in Miller that we did not.

Munro handed the old man a rifle and Miller sighted and worked the bolt like he'd carried the weapon for years and a few hours later calmly used it to expertly dispatch several outlaws who wished us the most severe sort of ill will.

But today Miller's placid façade had disappeared when he found a looter carrying bottles of laudanum through the broken window, which I hadn't had time to fix.

Stormy weather will put a man on edge and sometimes push you over it.

Miller was kicking the looter in the side. I didn't recognize the man; probably a cowhand or drifter who'd stopped in town to ride out the storm.

The looter would manage to get to his knees and scurry a few feet before Miller kicked him again, and then he'd splash back facedown into the water.

The pattern repeated about five times before I lost interest.

Here in the center of town the water had reached my shins and moved with a steady flow that, while not enough to knock you down, made forward motion difficult. Back at the bank, near the delta, it had reached waist height and was bubbling in animated torrents.

I had checked on the Spoon a couple of times in the morning and the doors were locked. I let myself in and spied on Elmira each time, and found her snoring away happily under about seven blankets. The window had cracked but did not shatter.

A little later, Carmody and I decided we would start a routine of splitting up and riding north and south along Front Street, our main thoroughfare. I went north, but kept my distance from the swirling waters of the delta, which were still rising.

On my way back, near the blacksmith shop, I found a man lashed to a tree with strips of leather.

I didn't know who he was, either.

"Why are you tied to a tree?" I asked him.

He flashed me an angry glower, though I thought I'd asked a perfectly polite and reasonable question.

"Hi Josiah," came a voice from inside the shed.

It was Richard Oak, the blacksmith. Oak was built like Hercules but didn't know much about guns or combat and, bless his heart, he'd once faced armed gunmen in my defense armed only with his pitiful little plinking rifle, a virtual toy that probably could not fell a squirrel big enough for Carmody's dinner.

"Caught him breaking in," Oak said, wiping his hands on a rag. "Not sure what he thought he'd steal but the wind tore my door open and blew it off its hinges."

I dismounted and walked inside. Oak's shop was flooded pretty badly; his shed had a dirt floor, unlike most buildings in town that were built up at least a few inches, mostly to boardwalk height or above.

"Sorry," I said. "You got hit pretty hard."

"It ain't bad, but thanks. The building's still intact, and nothing here is going to be damaged by some water. And dirt ain't like a floor. It won't rot because of the water. I might catch a cold from standing in it, but it's all good. In fact, I'm looking at a good couple of weeks because weather like this brings on a lot of bent wheel rims and horseshoes sucked off into the mud, not to mention busted hinges."

"Including your own," I said.

"Have that fixed in an hour," Oak said. "I'm firing up the hearth right now so I can heat it up and pound it out."

Oak raised his voice a little.

"And I'm going to get these pokers red-hot so I can torture that guy outside."

We were inside and out of view of the guy tied to the tree, who couldn't see that Oak had no pokers on the fire or elsewhere.

"Christ, ten of them," I said.

"The secret is that you keep rotating them so they never cool off."

"And you've got the *special* one. The one that fits right into the…well, you know, I don't like to think about it."

"Thanks for checking on me, Josiah. I can handle things from here."

I mounted up and ignored the increasingly desperate pleas from the guy tied to the tree.

Chapter 26

Carmody, who hadn't had as much to drink as I did the night before, agreed to spell me and let me lie down for an hour.

Elmira had awoken early and bitterly complained about the heat from the seven blankets and the fact that she'd bruised her face by walking into the wall when she got up from a bed that had somehow moved across the room on its own.

I didn't have the time or energy to explain.

On the way up to her bedroom I passed her at the bar. She'd opened up and was doing a fairly brisk business, although there was a half-inch of water on the floor and one of the walls was cockeyed.

Elmira spotted me and with the unerring instinct she had for determining I was too tired to function, decided that she wanted to talk.

She beckoned me into her back office and I answered her questions about the wind, the flood, Carmody's predictions, the seven blankets, the moving bed, and the trouble we'd had in the morning.

I asked her why she was dreaming about carrots and she looked at me like I was crazy. Maybe I was, crazy from exhaustion. *Beside myself*, as they say.

And then she kissed me and told me to lie down and promised not to bother me unless there was trouble.

I told her I hoped to hell there would be no trouble.

And, of course, right on cue, a bar-girl stuck her head in the door.

"There's *trouble,*" she said.

Chapter 27

There were three of them behind the bar. They were not only pouring themselves drinks but stuffing bottles into their pockets. One of them even pocketed a shot glass.

The tallest one, who sported a wild shock of red hair and a mask of outrage, which I suspect he wore perpetually, as part of his identity, looked at me, glanced at my badge, and asked me *what the fuck I wanted.*

What *I* wanted?

I told him I wanted him to stop stealing liquor and then submit to the beating I was going to lay on him.

For the second time in as many minutes I was getting a look that questioned my sanity and I was getting sick of it.

"Can't you see what's happening?" he said, waving a hand as though all the evidence he needed was right before my eyes and I was impossibly obtuse. "We been out in the rain and wind. It's a *disaster.* We is victims of a *disaster.* Least we is entitled to is a goddamn free drink."

I didn't quite see the connection between him getting wet and the presumed right to loot Elmira's bar, but I wasn't thinking clearly and the task of educating him step-by-step seemed daunting, so I took out my Colt and clubbed him over the head and he dropped straight down, coming to rest jackknifed on the floor with his face pressed against his knees.

The other two headed toward the door but kept the bottles.

"What," said one, a short man with a long beard that seemed to carry remnants of each of his last week's meals, "you gonna *kill* us because we need a drink?"

Something I never understood about the West, before I became part of it, was how much people read. During the war, a novel or a newspaper was a precious commodity. I'd even seen soldiers pore over the label on a box, over and over, just for something to occupy their eyes and mind.

I'd paid a premium for reading material during days when I was on the trail as a guard, or hunting rustlers. I remember paying several dollars for a book called Gulliver's Travels. I kept it for years, read it over and over, and eventually gave it to Carmody.

I knew enough of last century's British politics to get most of the jokes, which I believe the author hid in what you might mistake as a children's book so he could avoid repercussions, which back then could have meant the rack or the gallows.

One of the hidden jibes in the book was about how people who want things to work their way twist logic to claim moral superiority. It never ceased to amaze me how so many people I've encountered do just that – start from what they want and work backward for justification. Self-delusion has been used to justify mass homicide, slavery, and – several times this morning – the presumed right to take what's not yours because a catastrophe provided an opportunity.

And feel morally superior about it.

The man with the moldy beard was feeling superior. He raised his eyebrows and titled his head back.

"So," he said, infinitely satisfied with himself. "You gonna kill us for these bottles?"

"Yes," I said.

The hammer on my Colt makes an abnormally loud click when it's cocked. I don't know why, and it doesn't affect the function of the weapon, and in fact there are certain moments when it adds a little necessary drama to the situation.

They set the bottles back on the bar with infinite care, lining them up perfectly, and then they backed out, wide-eyed.

I dragged the redhead out by an ankle and left him in the street, where I assumed he'd either walk away when he awoke or be washed away by the current.

And then I dragged myself up the stairs and went to sleep, but not before I had the bad judgment to tell Elmira to wake me if there was more trouble.

I'd already heard the gunshots and was putting on my boots when she opened the door.

Chapter 28

"Carmody's already at the bank," Elmira said.

"What's happening?"

"Everybody's swimming in money," she said, her eyes wide.

I was annoyed. There was gunfire and I wasn't in the mood to decipher her obscure metaphors.

"Just tell me what's going on in plain English."

"They are swimming," she said, slowly, mouthing the words in exaggerated fashion as though I could get the point by reading her lips, and broadly pantomiming paddling motions. "In *money.*"

I gave up and let gravity pull me down the stairs two at a time. Pretty soon she'd start talking about carrots again.

It was a short walk but I elected to ride because I could scabbard my rifle and get an elevated view of whatever was going on.

The first object that came into view as I rounded the bend was Carmody firing that buffalo gun in the air.

"I'm going to build a new jail and put everyone one a you assholes in it forever if I have to," Carmody said.

I spurred the horse forward.

And then I saw it.

At least twenty people.

Fighting, snarling, swearing, gouging.

And swimming in money.

Chapter 29

The bank had been pushed off its foundations by more than twenty feet. The water continued to rush up against the back wall and formed a pool deep enough to swim in. Oddly enough, the fact that the river was effectively dammed up made the pool itself relatively calm.

The people were not calm. They clawed at what I first thought were lily pads, even though that thought made no sense. When I got closer I could see that what covered the lake were clumps of thousands of greenbacks, which made no sense either.

But it was happening.

In the middle of the melee was the owner of the grocery store. He was a rough man with meaty forearms and thick hands and was busily using them to club the owner of the dress shop, a woman who was in her fifties and a head shorter but who nonetheless fought like a wildcat and snarled like one, too. She wasn't quite tall enough to keep her head above water so she'd bob down from time to time and resurface, shake the hair out of her face, grab for more currency, and scratch at the grocer's eyes as he tried to reclaim what she'd snatched.

She tried to stuff it down the front of her dress but had an enormous bosom and didn't have much storage space and didn't appreciate the grocer's explorations for the money she did manage to stash.

There were kids fighting grownups, women fighting women, women fighting men, groups pitted against other coalitions, and three stray dogs who didn't have a human in the fight but circled the pool wild-eyed with joyful excitement.

Men reached underwater to jam the loot into their pockets and one, whose pockets were apparently full, stuffed some in his mouth.

Carmody fired another shot into the air.

"We could fire off a twelve-pound cannon and they wouldn't notice," I said.

Carmody looked at me and shrugged.

"I don't know what else to do. They're all going to kill each other. Jesus Christ, a lot of them is vagabond cowhands, but the rest is townsfolk. *Normal* people."

He shook his head.

"I thought they was normal, anyway."

The beefy grocer had lifted the dressmaker clear out of the water and looked to be trying to turn her upside down, apparently to shake her.

She kicked at him. She wore little pointed boots, so I imagine they hurt.

I knew her vaguely. Her name was Lamb or Lambert or something like that. I'd taken a theft complaint at her store once and I remembered her as being stiff and suffocatingly proper and always raising her eyebrows when she spoke.

"You cock*sucker*," she screamed, as the store keeper managed to invert her and pump like she was a salt shaker.

"You got any ideas?" Carmody said.

He was calm – he was always calm – but I could sense a little desperation in his demeanor.

Sometimes the exigency of a situation makes you think in ways you normally wouldn't. I'd improvised some pretty good strategy on the battlefield, if I do say so, when my life was on the line.

Right now, there may have been lives on the line, but not mine, and frankly at that point I didn't much care who lived and who died, as long as I could go back to sleep.

And that's when it hit me.

"It's *counterfeit*," I shouted.

It worked so well and so quickly I didn't know what to do next. They stopped caterwauling as sharply as a chorus when a conductor gives them the cut sign with his baton.

"It's...*evidence*," I shouted. *"Evidence.* It was seized in a raid and was going to be transported to federal authorities."

Carmody spoke up.

"You don't think we'd leave real money sitting in the bank knowing it was in the path of the delta water," he said. "We figured if something happened to this worthless shit nobody'd be dumb enough to think it was real."

I was afraid that he might have overplayed his hand because the grocer, who had certainly seen his share of greenbacks, began examining the wad clutched in his sausage-like fingers.

"Hold it up to the sky," I shouted. "Even though it's wet, you *can't see through it.* That's the giveaway. Real currency is made out of paper with…a *watermark."*

"Means that you put water on it and you can see the special symbols the government weaves in to show it's real money," Carmody said. "That's a law-enforcement secret but I believe considering the circumstances you have a right to know."

Sausage-fingers was holding up a bill to the slate-grey sky and shaking his head. Guess he'd never examined money soaked in water before. Not sure anybody had, anywhere, ever.

Some others scrutinized the bills up but most just looked down in defeat and disappointment and despair.

I waded knee-deep into the pool and held up my arms, preacher-style.

"Possession of those bills is a federal crime. I'm not trying to be a jerk about this, but I don't have any say in the matter. I have to put anybody holding counterfeit in jail and if I don't the feds will put me in jail with you. I will be powerless to protect you. And if they come looking for you they will show no mercy."

Carmody raised a fist.

"*None*! They offer no quarter! I seen what they did to people what got caught up by accident, just like you did. Federal prison. Making big rocks out a little rocks for twenty years."

The ones who didn't have wet hair hanging over their eyes looked at each other.

Carmody leaned forward and spoke to them in a conspiratorial stage whisper.

"Look, some of you seen the same thing I saw when I rode up. You seen Lovejoy the banker hightail out like his ass was on fire as soon as he saw that counterfeit floating around. Crying and flitting and whooping like a magpie the whole time. He's don't want no part of no federal prison. He's gonna turn you in as fast as he can find a federal marshal in Austin."

The dressmaker, who'd righted herself, raised a hand and reverted to her clipped and proper tones.

"What in heaven's name should we do?"

"Pick up every bill you can find," I said. "Don't think about keeping any of it because the government will put out an alert and if you so much as buy a sarsaparilla with it they'll find out. And then it's prison."

"Hard labor," Carmody declared. "Big rocks and little rocks."

"Playing checkers with somebody who killed the last person who beat him at checkers," I added, wondering, as I said it, if I were becoming delirious.

"You're getting delirious," Carmody whispered. "Go back to the Spoon and sleep it off. I'll handle this. The water's receding and we can't do much until we dry out. Tomorrow's cleanup day."

"Thanks," I whispered back. "First, I'll go get some feedbags from the hostler and drop them off and then you can stick the cash in the cell."

Carmody didn't take his eyes off the crowd but spoke to me softly without moving his lips too much.

"I didn't make up the part about Lovejoy. He rode out when I came in. He's probably ten miles away by now, and unless he runs his horse to death I doubt we'll ever see him again."

"The little prick has probably been stealing for years," I said. "A little at a time, not enough to be noticed, stashing it somewhere in his office. I'm guessing a phony wall or under a loose floorboard."

Carmody nodded slightly and addressed the crowd.

"Give me all the money," Carmody said. "I may get in trouble, but I'll take responsibility for it. Get every single bill off the surface of the water and put it in your pockets, and when you get to shore empty your pockets in front of me."

"I don't have pockets," said the dressmaker, "most quality dresses don't. And there's not that much...much *room* anywhere else."

Carmody apparently found that quite reasonable.

"I understand. Get as much as you can from the surface and give it to a man who has pockets."

She nodded primly and slapped a stack of wet bills against the chest of the grocer.

She hissed out her words.

"It's all yours, cocksucker."

Chapter 30

I slept like a dead man until dawn.

I'd gone lots longer without sleep during the war, and had suffered through more insistent hangovers, so I'm not sure why I'd been so exhausted.

But I felt good and only swore a little when I cracked my head on a shelf when I sat up. The bed was still in its oddball position against the opposite wall.

Elmira stirred a little when she heard me but went back to sleep. She was smiling. She really loved to sleep.

Some slanting light from the dawn caught the gold in her hair, along with counterpoints from a few fine strands of silver. Funny, I thought, how I always thought of her in metallic terms. She had a few wrinkles, to be sure, but to me they looked more like the fine lines on a face on a coin, not the claw marks I see gouged into the faces of so many people in the west, many of whom fled a hard life only to confront a harder one.

Elmira didn't know exactly how old she was. She'd been kidnapped as a young child and didn't keep careful track of intervening years, but her best guess was 42.

I decided to lie down for another couple of minutes until full daylight.

I'm 44 and am starting to feel it in strange ways. I'm almost as strong and quick as I ever was, but wear out faster. It's not just that I sleep a little more and lose some extra steam when I run or fight. I just get tired, mostly in the muscle between my ears. I run out of patience more easily.

It occurred to me that yesterday, when that asshole had asked me if I would kill him for brazenly looting the bar, I'd told him yes, which is the appropriate response for any lawman with a withering girlfriend-scaring scowl, and it worked.

He left without any further trouble, and I put out the fuse before the situation escalated.

But the problem was that it really brought home the fact that I'm getting tired of a lot of things, including assholes.

I wouldn't have killed him ten years ago, but yesterday I wasn't bluffing. I could have erased him and not felt any regret. And that scared me a little.

This morning maybe I wouldn't be so trigger-happy. You don't think clearly when you're tired, and maybe sliding deeply into middle age doesn't help the thinking process, either.

Maybe that was it. Age. I'd been tired and irritable lately, and have become increasingly forgetful.

I decided to stop thinking about it and get up and enjoy what looked to be a beautiful day.

And then I cracked my head on the shelf again.

Chapter 31

I don't favor flowery language but I had to admit that I could only describe the scenery as breathtaking.

The streets and some of the low-lying terrain were still flooded, but only by a half inch or so, and they caught the reflection of the clearest sky I ever recalled seeing.

Maybe it's like the old joke about the guy who's hitting his head against the wall and when asked for an explanation says he does it because it feels so good when he stops. It's just possible that three days of incessant rain and wind and assholes clawing for money in mudpuddles diminished my expectations and made an average sunny, so-far-idiot-free morning seem spectacular by comparison.

For a few minutes the world was a shimmering blue-and-green-and-gold paradise. Against the emerald hills, I could make out something that provided a beautiful scarlet counterpoint.

The spot of scarlet bobbed a little and I wondered if it were some exotic bird.

It was coming toward me, whatever it was, and in a couple minutes I could make out some vibrant points of snow white and charcoal black.

And then I figured out it was an Apache headdress and everything went to hell again.

Chapter 32

Taza said he was unhappy because twenty riders were on their way to kill me and he might not have the chance to do it himself.

The man held a grudge like glue.

Last year he'd been leader of an ambush party that got the drop on us. Carmody, who speaks enough of the language to get me into trouble, had calmed things down by insulting Taza on my behalf and telling him that even though I didn't look like much I could beat the Apache up like he was a little girl.

He goaded Taza into fighting me *mano-a-mano* with knives, under the provision that Carmody and I could go free if I won.

Which I did, thanks to the fact that I kicked Taza in the thigh and the big Indian fell forward and impaled himself on his own knife. Carmody insisted I kill Taza, that it was expected and the war party would kill me if I didn't follow through, but I didn't and they didn't and Taza has been singing the same song of revenge ever since.

Every time he saves my life he insists it's so he can do the job himself, and whenever I start to ask him for a favor he interrupts and tells me that if

I am asking for him to kill me quickly when the time comes, it will depend on how hard I beg.

Taza is nothing if not cagey. It turned out that Taza spoke English but hid the fact and knew what Carmody and I were planning while we spoke, secure in the assumption that we would not be understood.

Taza lectured me about falling for that trick.

And so did Carmody, who loves to lecture more than Taza does. The fact that Carmody fell for it too did not dampen his ardor as he recounted my strategic failings. Endlessly. With that finger stuck in the air.

Taza was unusually big for an Apache. Most were muscular but short; he had plenty of gleaming muscle but was well over six feet, almost as tall as Carmody. When he dismounts and talks with me he stands excruciatingly straight and tilts his head down to accentuate the inch or so he has on me.

"You are *fucked*," he said, looking as though he were trying to stifle a yawn.

He'd caught me languishing in my ten minutes of sanity and my mind wasn't working at full speed yet.

"Riders...where? You say there are about twenty men coming to kill me?"

"Not say 'about.' Apache is precise, not make sloppy guesses like you. Exactly twenty. Not broke camp yet, but coming this way before noon."

"How do you know they're coming to kill me?"

"I hear them talking. They say they going to kill 'dumb-shit marshal.' I do not know any other dumb-shit marshal."

I ignored him.

"Do you know who they are?"

"Do you know any *other* dumb-shit marshal? Maybe I make mistake."

"Do you know *who they are?*"

Taza turned thoughtful and decided to placate me with an answer.

"Gang thrown together. I watch for a while. Men stay in circles. Know people in their circles but ask others their names and don't talk much. Some look like what your ape deputy call 'down-and-outers.' Man in charge look like you probably look in few years, if I let you live that long. Grey hair. Gray beard. Mean eyes."

"Did he say anything else?"

"Mean face, too. Just like you. Look like mad at world all the time."

I decided to wait him out.

"He say dumb-shit marshal – that is you – kill his son."

Then Taza tilted his head, puzzled.

"He also say you know too much. You know too much *what*? Seem to me you do not know shit."

"That I can't tell you," I said. "I honestly don't know."

He nodded.

"We have maybe hour or two to figure out where to make stand against them," Taza said. "I come across them while hunting and know something strange going on. I listen for as long as I could, but figure best to sneak away and warn you. Not hear anything about their plans. They say nothing I hear other than ride into town soon and kill dumbshit marshal."

"I'm guessing they plan on staging something," I said. "Some sort of confrontation they can blame on me. Maybe claim self-defense. Maybe make it so no one knows for sure who fired the shot. You can get away with a set-up like that if you have money and lots of witnesses who will say what you pay them to say."

"They must move slow," Taza said. "Ground wet, some places they will not be able to pass, but they can pick way through like I do. They probably will follow same path I take this morning, hit flooded part, and have to double back like I do."

"We can't let them reach town," I said.

"No. Cassie's mother here."

I was surprised and almost said something, but thought better of it. Taza was married – I guess, we were never sure how the Apache arrangement worked, exactly – to Elmira's daughter. Cassie had gone insane from having too many horrible things to think about and too much time to think them, and when Taza "claimed" her I convinced Elmira that her daughter would be better off living a difficult life where thoughts about day-to-day survival fully occupied those haunted spaces in her mind.

I'd never heard Taza express concern about anyone's welfare other than mine, which he only expressed as a desire to preserve the opportunity to torture me at a later date.

I think it might have been a cultural thing.

But it didn't matter at the moment.

"Too many bullets," Taza said. "Too many people. Dumb-shit people like you, but still not good they die."

"You pick the spot," I said.

"I already pick spot. Trail look dry. But then the trail go through woods and runs into area flooded high as horse's head. *I* have to double back on way here and I know trails and ride better than those...what are those two words you always call people you do not like?"

"Thugs and goons."

"We ambush thugs and goons at flooded spot. You, me, deputy who look like ape, blacksmith with toy gun, and mean old man."

"You're talking about Miller, the druggist?"

"Mean old man with glasses who shoot thugs and goons in Canyon last time I save your...how do you people say it? Your *sorry ass*."

Chapter 33

Carmody, whose instincts about danger were unerring, showed up a couple minutes later. He told me he sensed something was up. He then told me he'd been at the Widow Dwinn's, and I changed the subject.

I stopped by the Spoon and went upstairs to Elmira's bedroom and left her a note saying I'd be gone on business and would be back later. The less said the better. And there was no need for dramatic goodbyes because she would remember nothing of any conversation that occurred before noon.

Miller was having difficulty installing a new window and seemed delighted to go on a probable suicide mission with me. He needed a gun, though. In a rare moment of candor he told me he'd sworn off guns after some unnamed incident and kept only an antique musket as a keepsake. When we pulled off an improbable rescue at the Canyon of the Long Shadows we'd provided him with a fancy German bolt-action that Major Munro had appropriated from somewhere or someone, and Miller had displayed a deadly accuracy with it.

I still had the German gun squirreled away in the office.

When I told him about it, the grim old man beamed. For him, apparently, this day suddenly could not get any better.

I caught Oak in mid-swing of his hammer. He dropped everything – literally – and told me he'd get his .22 and mount up. I told him we'd supply him with something that could actually shoot across an average-size street. He shrugged and nodded.

Oak had seen limited combat during the war and was a mediocre shot at best and knew nothing of tactics, but he also knew no fear whatsoever, and sometimes the willingness to gut it out is the best offensive weapon there is.

I'd put Taza in charge of rounding up the weapons and making sure we packed an appropriate stock of ammunition for each. Taza had done vigorous trading in guns, and while he wasn't a crack shot he knew firearms inside and out. I mean that literally: He possessed an encyclopedic understanding of what parts were interchangeable and what ammunition could be force-fit into a weapon not designed to accept it but still able to fire it with some coaxing.

Also, Taza was the only one among us who could make the key to my office door work the first time, and he also had a way with the endlessly fussy padlock that secured the chains through the trigger guards and levers of the rifles, so he was the natural choice to load us up.

Carmody and I walked over to the office where our mounts were hitched. Miller turned the corner riding his droopy gray mare. Normally I'd have insisted he switch horses, but we didn't need to go very far or very fast. Maybe Miller's horse would surprise me; maybe he had the same hidden reserve of energy as his owner.

Carmody and I both favored Steeldusts, quarterhorses that used to be metallic gray, hence the name, but now come in any old color. Over short distances they're as fast as anything that runs or flies – anything I've seen, anyway.

Oak was astride a very big Morgan, a thick-muscled brute that resembled Oak in the same manner as the droopy mare looked like Miller.

I was thinking how Taza looked a little like his athletic brown-and-white paint horse when I noticed his sour expression. Taza's expression, I mean, though the horse didn't look particularly happy either.

"Why you have pile of wet money in cell?"

"It's a long story, I said. "I'll tell you on the way."

"And why you have dead bodies rotting in corner of jail? Place smell like shit. *Worse* than shit. You have shit for brains."

"Shit," I said, repeating what I noticed had now become an exceptionally versatile all-purpose word. I'd forgotten about the two bodies that Old Man Carpenter had refused to claim. The hurricane, or whatever sort of storm it technically was, had diverted my attention.

"Shit," Carmody echoed. "I forgot about them bodies, too, what with the storm and all. We was gonna bury them but then Josiah decided to sleep for twelve hours and I was out and about enforcing the law while he was in a coma and never did go back to the jail. Slipped my mind."

I transferred a couple rifles to the scabbards on my Steeldust and mounted up.

I told Carmody that we'd bury the bodies when we got back.

I was going to say "if" we got back, but I don't like to be melodramatic.

And it looked like a warm day ahead, so getting killed or returning to dispose of the rotting bodies seemed equally distasteful, so I didn't much care either way.

Chapter 34

Taza led us to the spot he thought would lend itself as the site of an ambush, and then he turned the planning over to Carmody, who seemed to sense what a measure of respect it was for Taza to actually shut his mouth and defer to Carmody's almost supernatural understanding of terrain.

Of course, Taza's life was on the line, too.

We found the layout exactly as Taza had described it. A trail that descended a small mountain or a large hill – I never really knew the difference – wound through some dense woods and dead-ended at what had recently developed as an impromptu lake.

I asked Carmody what the odds were that the gunmen would follow this particular trail.

The odds were good, he told me. He knew the land between where the gunmen were camped and if he were coming to Shadow Valley, he would have followed the same route as Taza, not expecting the low-lying area to be so inundated.

If he were riding to Shadow Valley, he would reach the water and turn around and come down a longer trail about a half-mile to the east.

But, Carmody warned, he and Taza were experienced trailsmen and the choices they made would not necessarily be the ones made by Carpenter and his pickup goon gang.

The odds were in our favor, though. And when they entered the wooded trail – and when they doubled back after confronting the flooding – they'd be in a small valley with rocky hills on each side that would provide us excellent cover and allow us to pin them in a crossfire.

Taza nodded, as did Miller, Oak, and Carmody.

And then, to a man, they shook their heads in amazement when I told them I couldn't do it.

Chapter 35

"And since when has you become such a delicate flower?" Carmody asked. "The first time I worked with you, you wrung a sentry's neck and killed him on the spot just to keep him quiet. I thought you was the most cold-blooded man I ever did see. But now we got twenty men riding down on us and you're giving us a sermon on being kind to our fellow man."

"We were in the middle of the raid and outnumbered then, too," I said. "And Elmira's daughter was being held captive and the only way to complete the mission was to get rid of the sentry."

Miller rode a step closer to me.

"And what's different now?" he asked. I was surprised; it was a question, not an argument, and he posed it with no anger.

"First, we're not entirely sure that they're all coming with the purpose to kill me. I know Taza heard what he heard, and I'm not disputing that, but sometimes people say things that aren't literally true. All of us have said, 'I'll kill you,' and not meant it literally."

"From what I hear," Carmody said, "you said that yesterday to some down-and-outer who was trying to make off with a bottle of gin, and looks to most folks like you meant it. So you can gun somebody down for stealing cheap booze but not for coming to kill you?"

"To tell you the truth, I don't know if I would have. I might. But he'd been warned and knew the situation and would have brought it on himself."

Oak cleared this throat.

"Look, I'm not a lawman, and I've only shot at a few people and honest to God don't know if I killed them, but it seems to me it's either us or them. If we don't stop them, they'll go into town. I seriously doubt if they're just going to turn around and leave when they don't find the marshal, so we'll have to go in anyway. Why not do it on our terms where we have a chance?"

The man had a good point.

And then, so did Miller.

"What you say is true," Miller said. "And just among us, I want to say that I *have* killed, more than you can imagine. To the point where it didn't bother me. And then the fact that it didn't bother me bothered me more than you can imagine."

We'd nosed the horses into a rough circle and Miller looked each man in the eye in turn before he spoke.

"So I'm with Hawke," Miller said. "Killing in battle is one thing. Lots of people deserve killing. Probably most of these owlhoots deserve it for sure. But if we lie in wait and shoot fish in a barrel, we're committing an execution."

"Remember one thing," Carmody said. "I know the marshal is getting ready to serve us up some stuff about Aristotle and whatnot, but we is *way outnumbered*. Depending in the mettle of these guys, quite a few fish could get out of that barrel and flank us."

"I'm not bringing Aristotle into this," I said, "and I don't disagree with you either, but we're both sworn peace officers. We're not supposed to stage mass executions. I'm just not sure if the ends justify the means."

"That weren't Aristotle, anyway, professor," Carmody said, landing on the *perfesser* intonation with a little more sarcasm than I felt necessary. "More like Bentham: You do the right thing if what you do produces the greatest good for the greatest number."

Miller's glanced at Carmody, turned away, and seemingly unable to help himself, turned back again and stared.

"How the hell do you know this stuff?" Miller asked.

"I ain't no dummy," Carmody said.

When Taza spoke next, the deepness of his voice was a startling counterpoint to Carmody's Tennessee twang.

"I know all about idea that if it make most people happy it is right. But maybe most people *wrong* sometimes."

We were all silent for a minute and then Oak looked at Taza and shrugged.

"So, what do you want to do?

"When I first meet shit-for-brains marshal and ape-man deputy, they would have been easy kill. Still will be easy kill, when I get chance. But I do right thing and give marshal a chance to fight. Not expect he kick me in shin like little girl and run away, but I act like man, even if he act like little girl."

There was quite a bit more to it than that, but Taza is a proud man and I didn't see the need to quibble about details, especially when time was running out.

"Sometimes you do the right thing," I said. "Sometimes you come up with ways to justify what you're doing and pretend you're doing the right thing when you're just covering your own ass."

I dismounted and stepped to the edge of the trail snapped off a small branch from a dead tree.

"Marshal," Carmody said, "I have the truly horrifying dread you're going to kneel down and start to draw in the dirt with a stick again."

Chapter 36

For all his complaining, Carmody took three turns with the stick and four turns grinding out my lines with the toe of his boot.

And we came up with what looked like a pretty good plan. I say "pretty good" because there's an old saying among old soldiers that every plan looks foolproof until somebody starts shooting.

As the riders began cresting a hill, I snatched my spyglass from the saddlebag and scanned the array of mounted men apparently determined to kill me.

Twenty men was a lot.

But there were twenty, exactly twenty, and that was good. No strays. No flankers approaching from an unexpected angle. At least not yet.

I located Carpenter. He was in the middle of the pack.

The pack itself was a motley collection, and I think Taza had it right – they were a pick-up gang. From the way the horses were grouped, they were split up into three phalanxes. Carpenter's group were dressed in good-quality rancher's clothes. To the right, a knot seemed to be of cohesive background, a group of down-and-out cowhand types looking to pick up easy money. To the left were stragglers. One man wore overalls. Another a tattered suit, presumably from a more prosperous life lived at a time when conditions were better. Three or four in the straggler phalanx wore sombreros and sported their ammunition belts crossed over their chests, Mexican-style.

They'd see me in a minute. I'd make sure of that, even though I was uphill and far to the left of the route they planned to take.

I collapsed the spyglass and edged the Steeldust closer to the bank of the river. Then I took out the hand-mirror I use for signaling back and forth to Carmody and pointed it toward the pack.

It took a good five minutes for one of them to notice. One rider in sombrero pointed in my direction, and the pack halted. Then Carpenter advanced toward me, and the rest formed into the type of V formation that follows the lead bird.

I waited until they got to shouting distance but not quite to comfortable shooting distance – about two hundred yards. Somebody who took careful aim with a rifle could hit me, but it wasn't an easy quick shot from horseback.

I shouted for them to stop.

Carpenter held up a hand, and while I couldn't read his expression clearly, he seemed cautious and puzzled.

So far, so good.

"Do you all speak English?" I shouted.

The question caught them by surprise, which is what I intended. I didn't give a damn if they spoke Greek or Latin, but I needed their attention and the surest way to get it is to feed them something that makes them wonder why you're asking.

No one nodded or said anything but they all looked right at me.

"Good," I said. "I don't know who you are or what your reasons are for signing up with Carpenter, but I know you're supposed to kill me."

I scanned a horizon of eyes of flint.

"I'm not going to tell you about the penalty for killing a peace officer," I said, noticing that the breeze had picked up and hoping my words would carry. "I'm not going to tell you that if you ride down at that town innocent people will be hurt. I know none of that matters to you."

I reined the Steeldust into a slow walk and moved sideways. We were a bigger target facing sideways but a walking horse can make a bolt faster than one standing still.

"What I *am* telling you is that if you try it you will *die*. If you turn around now, I'm not promising I won't kill you someday, or at least throw you in jail, but you'll get to go home tonight."

They could hear me. The acoustics were better than I thought because I could very plainly hear them laugh.

"And I view an attack by one of you as an attack by all," I said. "Meaning that you'll all pay the price if one of you raises a weapon."

"Like this?" asked a lanky kid wearing a mean expression and stained buckskins as he slid his rifle out of a scabbard.

Sound is funny. Maybe it was the hills on both sides or the reflection off the water, but I could hear the faint hiss of the metal sliding on the leather.

Funny, too, how sound is so slow, lagging behind a high-velocity round fired from a distance.

I heard the slapping sound of the slug tearing into the side of his skull and observed the man next to him being pelted by a shower of bright crimson before the crack of the buffalo gun echoed through the hills.

Chapter 37

I opened up with my Henry rifle. It's a lever-action weapon that I'd used in the war and liked. Other rifles might be more accurate or carry a more powerful load, but nothing else you can carry in your hand lets you unleash a world of hurt in such short order.

The point was to put them back on their heels for a minute and allow me a running start. At that distance I didn't really expect to hit anybody.

I'm the first to admit, though, that luck plays a role in gunplay. I saw two of them fall before I turned and spurred the Steeldust.

I didn't look back. Looking back slows you down. I don't know how, and I know it doesn't make sense, and any scientist could go to a chalkboard and prove me wrong in theory, but I know what I know. And I hunkered down with my head against the withers to make myself a smaller target. I couldn't shrink the horse but keeping its butt squarely facing the pursuers at least made the target area as small as possible.

A galloping horse makes a lot of noise but I could hear some of what was unfolding in back of me.

The sound of Carmody's rifle continued to pound away. He was using a .50 caliber Sharpes, the kind used for hunting bison, and while it wasn't a fast-firing weapon it was accurate at long distance and Carmody could reload and fire so fast it was like a magic trick.

There was also considerable splashing and cursing and some horse-sounds that I took to be the equine version of cursing. Carmody had somehow known that the stream that separated me from the gunmen was deceptively deep and had flooded to the point where the horses would have to swim.

Horses are actually pretty good at swimming but they have to be introduced to the water gradually.

Horses are *terrific* at panicking if they can't find footing and the water comes up to their heads.

These weren't trained cavalry horses. They snorted and flailed and turned back to shore.

I heard someone – it might have been Carpenter – shout "this way," and there were hoofbeats in the distance. It seemed safe to risk a glance over my shoulder now and the riders were doing just what Carmody had predicted – moving to their right trying to find a shallow ford. Half of them were scrutinizing the stream and the remainder were eyeing the hills with rifles pointed trying to find the source of the gunfire.

One of them spotted Carmody's smoke and they opened fire.

Carmody, of course, would be a quarter-mile away by now, riding a high trail and working his way to the spot where we'd kill the rest of them.

Chapter 38

I almost lost them, so I slowed down.

The last thing I wanted was to let them lose sight of me. At the same time, I didn't want to let them get too close. There were probably thirteen or fourteen of them left and while it would have been a damn lucky shot to hit me firing from horseback, one shot was all it would take.

I followed along the edge of a long sloping hill, the route they'd take once they got past the swollen stream.

Which they did. I could see horses shoot out single-file from what looked to be a narrow ford. They popped out of the foamy water steadily, almost like they were being poured from a faucet.

That made my escape easier. They'd be spread out from front to back and while some horses would be faster than others and eventually pack up with the rest, I'd only have the leaders nipping at my heels for a while.

I actually had to slow the Steeldust down, which wasn't easy because I think he sensed we were being pursued and he couldn't figure out my baiting tactics. I tugged back ever so slightly on the reins – maybe becoming the first man in all of recorded history to do so while being pursued by an armed gang.

Everything depended on them keeping me in sight. Actually, for me, everything depended on not getting shot, but I had to keep them fairly tight on my trail.

I heard four rifle cracks, but didn't hear any bullets buzz by or see the ground chewed up to my left or right.

I grabbed my shoulder and made a show of fighting to stay on my mount.

It occurred to me that should any of my pursuers have much experience or training in riding they could catch on to the fact that my mount had run like lightning a few minutes ago but was intentionally being slowed. That, of course, would make them wary and I didn't want them wary: I wanted them drunk with the rage of closing in on a kill.

If they bought my act it would explain why I was losing a little momentum. A wounded man loses coordination and balance and as a result his mount loses a stride or two.

So I rode with my right arm limp at my side.

The trail into the woods was a few hundred yards ahead; I recognized the passage because of the lighting-struck tree to the right and the twin slopes rising on either side.

Some of them probably knew the trail. Carpenter surely would, and if the others were local they'd probably come through it often. But I didn't know if Carpenter was in the lead. I wanted to leave nothing to chance so I took my time posing in the opening of the passage.

I allowed myself the luxury of one last look behind.

Carpenter was in the lead. But he'd pulled up and was waving riders in back of him on with circular arm motions and pointing toward me with his rifle.

The riders pounded past Carpenter and rode down on me.

I hesitated for a second, curious as to why Carpenter was waving them past. Maybe he'd chickened out, and figured the hired help should do the shooting. Or maybe he was afraid the riders toward the back would lose the trail if he didn't hang and point them in the right direction.

Or maybe he sensed that something was up.

Chapter 39

W^e were about a quarter mile from the deep water.

         I spurred the Steeldust and rode low.

He was happy and began to pick up speed like a locomotive heading down a mountain.

A quarterhorse – mine, anyway – can cover that distance as fast as any thoroughbred racehorse. They're bred to excel at that distance, hence the name of the breed.

I was as happy as my horse because I was doing what, apparently, I was bred to do.

As sometimes happens when I'm gearing up for battle I think about things that make me happy.

I thought about Elmira's gold-and-silver hair and about a recent conversation we'd had about quarterhorses in which she'd told me she'd thought it meant they were quarter-sized. As mine stood more than 16 hands – and was towering right before her eyes when she said it – I wondered where, exactly, she expected all the normal elephant-sized horses were hiding.

I was laughing out loud when I hit the water.

The Steeldust let out a snarl and when the water reached his girth he stretched out his front legs in a diving motion, as happy as a kid plunging into a swimming hole.

I plucked my rifle from the scabbard and held it high while I reined the horse around and he paddled so I was facing the shore.

It was almost like shooting from a boat, but I was able to keep my bearings when the first pursuer came into view.

He drew back when he saw the water and the strange horse-paddling gunboat and tried to bring his rifle to his shoulder but I killed him before he'd raised it more than a couple inches.

There was a scuffling commotion in back of him as riders reined their mounts, again confounded by the unexpected body of water.

I spied another rider who'd drifted into my view. He was confused, and instead of raising his sights on me he tried to turn around but his horse's head butted up against another mount that had pulled up alongside.

Both men looked at each other, startled, and one started to angrily shout and wave before I shot him in the side of the head.

The other gunman looked straight at me. He knew he was going to die, seemed resigned to it, in fact, so I obliged and drilled him in the middle of his forehead.

I guess that the trail had filled up with the remaining riders because Carmody, Miller, Oak, and

Taza – who had been holding their fire until they were sure they had everyone penned in – opened up from the hills on either side, cutting them down in less time than it took my horse to paddle to shore.

Chapter 40

I did feel bad about the horses. One of the gunmen's mounts was wounded and I had to put it down, and another was killed outright from a shot to the back of its head. From the angle, it appeared to me that it happened when one of the gunmen was drawing his revolver in a panic.

There's a lot of what you might call awkward moments in the aftermath of a gunfight. There were twelve dead men here, presumably a few in the field where we'd had our first encounter, and at least one who had escaped.

The escapee, of course, was cagey Old Man Carpenter.

Anyway, we had bodies and horses and property on our hands.

During the war the disposal of bodies had become a paramount issue. I'm no historian, but from what I've read I believe that in smaller-scale confrontations in the past there was a great deal of ceremony attached to internment of the dead. During the war, we didn't have that luxury. In places like Gettysburg, Chickamauga, and Shiloh there were more bodies than the living population of some good-size cities, and even in smaller battles we'd wind up with more dead that we knew what to do with.

Mass graves were often a necessity, and it looked like that's what we'd have to settle for here. In a lawman's perfect world, my staff of assistants would take to the hills and track down next of kin and arrange for burial of each and every body and dispose of property accordingly. But in Shadow Valley and environs that was not only a vision of perfect world but an outright fantasy world, so we settled for burying them in four shallow holes and covering them with enough dirt that it would keep the animals from getting to them, at least for a while.

We didn't have any shovels – I hadn't thought to prepare for casualties, even those involving me, except for leaving Elmira a note – but Taza and Carmody cut down branches and fashioned sharpened digging sticks to loosen up the soil and used flat rocks to scoop it out. Oak, the brawny blacksmith, could dig like a badger.

Miller helped as much as he was able in the digging and advised on the planning of the holes. He seemed to have an unusual depth of knowledge on the subject of the proper depth of graves.

I was going to ask him about it but figured it was something I didn't want to pursue, and he probably didn't, either.

The property was another dilemma. Horses can usually do fine on their own, and I considered just scattering them. Most were just as motley and woebegone as the drifters who'd ridden them, so Carmody and I had no use for them and while I suppose we could have made a few dollars for the town coffers by selling them, it didn't seem worth the trouble.

Taza said he could use them, and that was fine with me. I suspected they'd wind up as trade items, maybe for a gun that could someday be used against either a white man or a Comanche, but they could also be traded for farm implements or other necessities of life.

Again, I chose not to ask too many questions.

The guns and ammunition I kept. Not that they were weapons I'd actually consider using – the rifles and sidearms were generally of a lower standard than the horses – but it's asking for trouble to leave firearms around, even in shallow graves.

There was a pathetically small amount of cash and other possessions. We searched through the saddlebags before turning the horses over to Taza, who would drive them as a pack back to his village. I'd keep the collection of belongings for a while, on the off-chance that somebody, somewhere, would appear and inquire about the property of one of the dead men.

I packed up the belongings as we interred the bodies. There were several wallets, two bibles, and maybe fifty dollars in bills and coins.

Carmody finished up interring the last body and handed me what he'd taken from the dead man's pockets, telling me to keep this property separate from the rest.

In his right hand he held a substantial but simple wallet.

From his left dangled another of the goddamned brass pocket watches.

Chapter 41

We'd arrived home well after dark and the first thing I did was to track down Elmira at the Spoon.

She surprised me by hugging me and burying her face in my chest.

Carmody had somehow managed to brief her on what had happened while I was putting my horse up at the hostler and depositing the guns and other property at the office.

The office visit took longer than expected because I had to keep ducking out for air. I'd forgotten about the bodies in the corner. I almost threw up.

Elmira was crying. Heaving, in fact, in one of her jags that leaves her gasping for air.

When she finished, she pulled out a handkerchief, dabbed daintily at her eyes, and then dragged her sleeve along her nose with snort that I would have more likely expected from Carmody.

"I didn't know there was a gang gunning for you," she said.

"There's pretty much always somebody gunning for me, and as it turned out this bunch wasn't that much of a threat."

I waited for it but it never came – the subtle repudiation where she slyly implies that I'm a mass murderer. And this time, she might have a case.

"Carmody told me that you'd staged it up in the hills to keep them from coming into town. He said you'd mentioned me."

I nodded but didn't say anything. Trying to keep innocent people, including her, from getting killed is common sense. And as it turned out, baiting them into following me had been more deadly than any stand in the home streets could possibly have been.

But I was glad that she understood, or at least pretended to understand, that I didn't gun people down for fun.

She reached up and plucked off my hat.

"No new holes."

"Nothing came close," I said, and it was true.

She placed my hat back on my head and patted it down.

"Just another day at the office," she said.

"Let's not talk about the office," I said, swallowing hard and moving toward the bar.

Chapter 42

The next morning I fiddled with the lock longer than necessary, took a deep breath, and plunged into the combination office/mortuary.

It didn't smell like a rose garden, but the overpowering stench was gone.

And the bodies were gone, too.

Everything else was in order, including the huge pile of cash in the cell, so I could only assume that Carmody was bestowing an act of mercy on me.

I am not, by any measure, a squeamish man, but putrefying corpses do make me pause to get my digestive tract working in the right direction. One of the first cases I'd faced here I solved with the aid of slugs dug out of the brain of Billy Gannon. Carmody dug up the body and pried them out for me, a task I imagine I would have put off until the day I was occupying the plot next to Gannon.

So I left the door open, opened the window, and settled in for a busy morning.

First, I counted the cash in the cell. It looked like more than it was because a lot of it was in small denominations, but it still came to $9,431. I drafted the text of a telegram to the Austin headquarters of the bank informing them that their bank had been moved off its foundations, their manager had fled, and that I had $9,431 in their counterfeit money.

I figured I'd explain the counterfeit reference when bank officials arrived. I'd never completely trusted the old weasel at the telegraph office and the last thing I wanted was for townsfolk to catch on to the fact that the money was real.

I'd drop the draft at the telegraph office when it opened. In the interim, I made some more coffee and congratulated myself for not pocketing any of the money, which would have probably been a completely undetectable crime unless Lovejoy was captured and confessed to embezzling exactly $9,431.

Which, actually, was not unthinkable given his fastidious nature and tendency toward hysteria.

So I congratulated myself again and moved on to the unopened mail.

I laid the circulars about the train robberies flat on my desk. There were six of them, and with them all arrayed I was able to discern some patterns, as could pretty much anybody who bothered to actually read them.

But there were no trains in Shadow Valley, and as even the idea of one coming here had caused considerable ruckus in the past, so I just couldn't summon up much interest. Besides, the train line, the Pinkertons, and the state were fully staffed by people who could stare at six pieces of paper on their desks with similar efficiency.

In addition to the circulars, there was the usual influx of wanted posters, most of them not of much interest. I'm not saying it doesn't happen, because it does, but the odds of spotting someone randomly are pretty steep, and while the rewards are tempting more often than not you'd have to deliver the prisoner in person after a tense ride that could take a week or longer.

And then there were letters. Official stuff in surprising amounts comes to both me and Carmody and almost none of it is of much interest.

I almost tossed away an official-looking, week-old letter with a state seal until I saw that Tom Harbold had written in his name below the return address. Harbold is a constable in Austin who'd been part of the mission we'd staged at the Canyon of the Long Shadows, where we'd rescued the daughter of a judge and, as usual, plunged into endless complications that ended in unexpected violence.

The envelope was flamboyantly embossed and the stationery had so much fancy lettering at the top, listing a litany of politicians and appointees, that Tom's neat printing didn't start until almost halfway down.

"Thought you'd want to see this – more railroad shit, I believe, down your way," the handprinting said. That was all. I was perplexed for a minute but then my advanced law enforcement instincts kicked in and it occurred to me to look in the envelope again.

It was a newspaper clipping, just about one by two inches, and at the top Tom had written in bright blue ink, AUSTIN EVENING NEWS, SEPT. 12, 1877.

It read:

A shooting affray occurred Tuesday morning in the town of Fort McCoy, growing out of a confrontation between several local men and a shooter named Henry Best, who those witnesses allege is a hired gunfighter. Witnesses say Best provoked the men, who had apparently been involved in a dispute involving a land claim, and killed three in rapid succession. Best left town and his whereabouts are unknown. There are no charges pending against him.

Fort McCoy is about 20 miles northwest. I'd been there only once, and it wasn't much to look at and in fact didn't have a fort, or even the vestiges of one, as far as I could see. What it did have, apparently, was some land that somebody thought was going to become valuable.

After re-reading the article, I couldn't help but conclude that the news is basically the same thing happening to different people.

There was one more letter, this from the mayor's office in Copper Ridge, about 25 miles west. I'd never been there, and had no idea why the mayor would write me and tell me that a job offer was still open, nor did I remember that he'd offered me a job in the first place.

I looked at the envelope, which I hadn't bothered doing when I opened all the letters at once in my early-morning spurt of ambition.

And then I looked at the opening salutation of the letter, which I'd skipped over, too.

It was addressed to Carmody.

Only one good thing came out of the three days of drenching rain that had inundated Shadow Valley. It had been so insufferably humid that the stamps had fallen off several of the envelopes and the glue that held the flap closed on this one was barely tacky and the flap hadn't been ripped when I opened the letter.

So I licked it and re-sealed it. It didn't stick any better than the first time but I didn't think Carmody would notice when I gave it to him, jammed in the middle of the rest of the mail that had fossilized in my drawer during the storm.

Chapter 43

I crossed paths with Carmody several times during the day but didn't have much time to talk until about eight, when we both were on duty at the Spoon. Our duties consisted mainly of dealing Faro when the spirit moved us, which was infrequent, and drinking, a responsibility we took seriously.

I bought Carmody a bottle of expensive whiskey as partial payment for burying the bodies. I told him that I damn near was ready to kiss him when I found they no longer were decomposing in the corner.

He told me that if I ever tried to kiss him he would dig up the bodies and personally put them in my bed and force me to copulate with them at gunpoint, although he phrased it less delicately. So I dropped the subject.

Carmody then pulled cork out of the whiskey bottle and poured himself a shot.

"Don't have much of a bite," he said, pondering the aftertaste.

"Probably because it's real whiskey and not that embalming fluid you drink."

"Thanks all the same," he said, and regarded me thoughtfully as he drummed his fingers and then poured another shot. "It *is* smooth. Like sodee pop."

More drumming.

"Something's on your mind," I said.

"Couple things," Carmody said. "I went through the mail you left me."

I tried not to react.

"I saw the article Harbold sent. About Henry Best. You heard a him?"

I tried not to show relief.

"I've heard a little. Gunfighter, travels around the South. Not much known in these parts."

"I heard a him," Carmody said. "He was known in my parts before I came West. Very well-known."

"Meaning?"

"Meaning you know that gunfighter Purcell who damn near killed you before you got off a lucky shot with your left hand?"

That's not exactly the way it happened but I was anxious for Carmody to get to the point so I nodded.

And that gunfighter Tremaine, who was faster than Purcell, and plugged you in the shoulder before you got off that lucky shot after you'd fell flat on your ass?"

That actually was a little closer to the truth, although I did go to the ground on purpose, but I let it pass, too.

"So?"

"So this guy's more dangerous than both of them put together. He's a heavy hitter, and don't come cheap. If we're being drawn into something like last time it's serious business. You just might run out of rabbits you can pull out of your dumb farmer hat."

"You think it might have something to do with the railroad business again? Some secret plans for a new route that's making the wolves lick their chops? Trying to squeeze in and buy up property before the plans become public and the value shoots up by a hundred times?"

"Could be that or any one of a dozen things," Carmody said, "But I wouldn't rule out nothing."

He seemed to be gathering his thoughts and I knew something was coming.

"Something else I gotta tell you."

It occurred to me that I hadn't decided how I was going to react if Carmody took the job. Or if he didn't. Whether it would be good news or bad news or a combination.

"I know this is awkward," Carmody said.

"Yes?"

"But the Widow Dwinn's coming to the Spoon tonight."

I experienced a momentary relief and then realized that I had no reason to be relieved.

"Tonight?"

"Christ, Josiah, it ain't like Henry Best is pointing a gun at your head. Yes, in about an hour. Insists on riding in herself. Very independent woman. She's done stuff you wouldn't believe a woman could do – just about every type of job you could imagine. Cattle drives, carpentry, card dealer..."

"That's, well, *wonderful.*"

"I know you and Elmira is the most gracious folk in the world, but I was just wondering if you could go special out of your way to make her feel at home. She's got what you might call *different ways.* A little rough. Sometimes she says stuff a little too direct for most people's tastes. She don't mean no harm."

"Of course not," I said.

Carmody smiled.

"Yep, some a the stuff that comes outta her mouth, well you can barely believe it. She can get on your nerves sometimes, but I tell you the truth, Josiah, you never knowed *nobody* like her."

"Nobody," I lied.

Chapter 44

I relaxed a little, partly on account of the fact that I was winding down from a natural disaster, survived a battle that claimed nineteen lives, not including mine, and, most importantly, didn't have to immediately confront the fact that Carmody might be leaving.

Also, before Carmody started sucking the expensive whiskey I'd bought for him right out of the bottle I'd felt justified in sneaking a few pours, and it was very good. Not at all like *sodee pop*, I thought, but it sure was smooth, and it stoked a comforting fire in my belly.

I played some war ditties and a cowpoked version of a Mozart sonata.

While he awaited the landing of the Widow Dwinn, Carmody resumed his study of the watches that we'd been collecting from corpses.

There were four of them now, including the one Nonie had recovered from the killing field. She kept in in her apron pocket but lent it to Carmody for the purpose of him staring at it.

Old Man Carpenter still had his.

The one we'd taken most recently did not belong to a Carpenter. It was engraved TM.

Carmody had them all face-up, lined up a neatly as museum exhibit.

I noticed that he'd wound them, and Nonie had apparently kept hers wound, because they all registered 9:03.

They were handsome devices. The numbers were large, elegant, and clear against a snowy white face. Right underneath the 12 was the word "Elgin," and where the six would normally be there was a circle with a second hand.

The second hands looked to be keeping time within about 30 seconds of each other.

"Sure wish I knew what I was looking at and why I was looking at them," Carmody mused, holding his chin in both hands.

"Maybe we're reading too much into this," I said. "Maybe they were stolen."

"Knowing Carpenter I don't doubt that for a second, but why wouldn't they just sell them? Why carry them around? Get them engraved? What's so all-fired important to a bunch of crooks about pocket watches?"

Carmody and I both jumped as the batwings swung inward and slapped loudly against the inside walls.

I involuntarily moved my hand near my revolver.

As peaceful as a bar can seem in relaxing moments, the mixture of alcohol, transients, and firearms makes for constant potential volatility.

Sometimes trouble comes through the door quickly, loudly, when you least expect it.

"*Heyah, Tommy,*" hooted the Widow Dwinn, her enormous wingspan still pinning the batwings against the wall.

Chapter 45

She strode clear across the room in about four steps and slapped me on the shoulder and said hello and then did the same to Elmira, setting Elmira off balance a little, even though Elmira was sitting, and then offered her hand to Carmody palm-down, elegantly, in a gesture one would expect from a French countess.

Carmody took her hand and held it in both of his for a second.

Elmira's eyes started to bug out again as she stared at the clutch of huge hands a couple of inches away from her nose. The Widow Dwinn's hand plus two of Carmody's were about the size and contour of your average cavalry saddle.

Dorothea Dwinn broke her adoring gaze with Carmody and looked down at the display of watches on the table.

"Where'd you get them?" She asked. It came out, *warhd ya git thim?* It was the same general melody as Carmody's twang, but clearly of different origins. I placed it somewhere around Kentucky.

Carmody chuckled.

"Just a mystery, Dorothea. Some evidence what turned up and we cannot fit the pieces together."

Dorothea spread her hands – again, an impressive sight, sort of like a condor taking flight.

"What the hell's so mysterious about a bunch a railroad watches?" she asked.

Chapter 46

Usually I take my hat off indoors but in the military I got out of the habit and I was wearing it when Dorothea identified the watches.

If I hadn't worn the hat, I would have slapped my forehead.

"Why didn't *you* think a that?" Carmody said, looking like he wanted to slap my forehead too, leaving unspoken the question of why he didn't think of it himself.

"I don't know much about railroads," I said.

Carmody nodded.

"Evidently."

Dorothea, as it happened, knew *everything* about railroads. She'd been a nurse of sorts on passenger trains and troop trains during the war; passenger trains sometimes carried onboard nurses and Dorothea said she was pretty good at pulling people out of wrecks and resetting dislocated shoulders and the like.

She'd later worked on cleaning crews, which were primarily staffed by women who Dorothea said were valued for the feminine touch they brought to the trains and stations. Before getting into ranching with her late husband, she'd also done a stint cleaning the trains' air brakes. I don't know what an air brake is or why it would get dirty, and urged her to get to the point.

She took a pull right out of Carmody's expensive bottle of whiskey and drained it. I bought her another. I would have bought a case of whiskey to get to the bottom of the damn watch business.

The devices were made by Elgin, she told me, which I could have figured out because it was printed on the dial. But there was more: These were "railroad grade" watches designed by a fellow named B.W. Raymond. While the definition of "railroad grade" varied according to the specifications of the individual train line, it basically meant that the watches were all certified to be accurate within a couple of seconds each month. They also had to have a certain number of jewels and usually had to have a time-setting mechanism different from the winding mechanism so that there was no chance of the hand position being accidentally changed when the spring was wound.

A railroad would buy the watches, or sometimes compel their employees to buy a certain brand of watch, and one person would be in charge of making sure they all met certain specifications and would conduct regular inspections to assure that they were not damaged and keeping time properly.

The watches were often engraved with the initials of the person who used them, not out of sentimentality but to keep track of whether all watches had been inspected regularly and that the employee didn't sell or gamble away the watch, replace it with a cheap one, and borrow a co-worker's come inspection time.

Accuracy of time was literally a matter of life and death on the railways, Dorothea explained as she guzzled the second bottle, because which train headed in what direction and at what time was all predetermined according to an intricate schedule, and if a conductor was off by so much as a minute it could mean two trains headed in opposite directions on the same track crashing head-on, or colliding at a crosswise intersection.

I asked her where someone could buy railroad watches. The answer was basically anywhere. They weren't particularly expensive because they were made of common metal, and the Elgins, at least, were mass-produced. Almost anyone who sold watches could do the engraving, as could most gunsmiths, some blacksmiths, and anyone handy with a hand-graver or small chisel. Anyone with any experience in railroading would know the approved brands and movements and how to set up an inspection system.

I didn't ask why a collection of thugs and goons would want railroad watches. The fact that anyone with an accurate watch and timetable could predict the location of a train anywhere in the state at any given time and could therefore plan an organized system of robberies would be clearly evident to most of the higher apes. Now that I'd been given a primer on the subject, I actually understood it my-self.

Chapter 47

I had trouble staying awake at my desk the next day. I'd left for Austin well before dawn – 4:46 a.m., to be precise, which I could be, now that I had an entire collection of railroad watches at my disposal.

I'd spent the morning collecting every railroad timetable I could lay my hands on and talking to a Pinkerton and a couple other law enforcement types of my acquaintance who'd worked as railroad police.

I didn't get much from the Pink, who seemed to regard local marshals as amateurs and interlopers who didn't know much about railroading. He was certainly correct about the latter part of that assessment, at least in my case.

The railroad police were a different breed. I knew two constables who'd worked at one time for railroads, and they were big, rough, and ruthless. At various times in their careers they'd lent their skills to pursuits on both sides of the law.

They knew about the recent robberies, of course, and filled me in on several incidents of which I had not been aware, including sabotage that had led to four separate wrecks, and some mysterious problems with signals that had led to a series of near-misses.

But they were skeptical – as was the Pink – about my theory that the incidents were somehow connected. The distances were too great for one enterprise to carry off, they said. The idea that incidents in San Antonio and Austin could serve as diversions to one another was possible, they surmised, but far-fetched. And there was no apparent relationship between the sabotage and the robberies. Why would anyone intent on robbing trains squander time and effort on crashing them with no apparent profit motive?

I didn't have an answer to that.

Yet.

I tried to think about it on the way back, but got caught up in trying to extricate myself and the Steeldust from a series of mudholes. The trail I took up was still wet and impassible in places, so I tried a different trail home, which turned out to be even worse.

When I made it back I was more or less dry but covered in caked mud and must have looked like a walking clay statue.

Elmira offered to wash my shirt and pants along with some linen from the bar, and I changed up in her room and washed up a little. I still keep lodgings at the hotel even though I spend most nights with Elmira, and keep most of my clothes at the hotel. All I had at the Spoon was a pair of ratty pants and a long-sleeved undershirt. I wanted to get into the office to think brilliant thoughts as quickly as possible, so I threw on what was available.

So that's why I was sitting at my desk, dressed like a hobo, at 4:13 – precisely 4:13, mind you – studying maps and timetables when Bill Liddicoat strutted in.

Chapter 48

Liddicoat wasn't a pompous asshole, exactly, but seemed to be sort of a pompous asshole-in-training.

He'd been sent by the bank to check on the $9,431 sitting in my cell. Someone else, he informed me, would be by to handle the fact that the bank was off its foundations and sitting cockeyed a fair distance from where it was originally built.

Liddicoat wasn't the bank examiner type. He was my size, rangy, and wore black clothes and a holster slung low in the style favored by the types who fancy themselves gunfighters and wear their iron where it's hard to reach just to show they are in fashion. He regarded my hobo outfit with obvious disdain and kept fussing with the precise knot it the bandana he wore.

Liddicoat had a badge, a dull shield-shaped model engraved with one word – "OFFICER" – but carrying no other ornamentation.

It's no harder to get a badge than it is a railroad watch so I pressed him on exactly what his position was with the bank and he told me "fixer."

That sounded like an honest answer to me, but I asked for identification, which he presented, and, of course, which any printer could have confected.

Liddicoat did know the circumstances of the case, and seemed to quickly grasp the reason I'd referred to the money as counterfeit, but that information could be gleaned from the weasel at the telegraph office, so I told Liddicoat that I'd answer his questions, which I did, but would not turn over the money to him until I or my deputy had ridden to the bank's main branch near Seguin and verified his identity. Then he could come back and get the money. I wanted no part of transporting the cash myself, I told him, because lately I had become ambush-bait.

I was 99 percent sure he was for real and it made perfect sense that a tough pompous asshole-in-training would be sent to investigate an embezzlement case and shepherd back a huge sum of money, but I wasn't $9,431 sure.

Liddicoat got huffy and stood up.

"Do you know who I am?" he asked.

No, I told him, and that was precisely the problem.

He didn't have a snappy answer to that so he stomped out.

He left the door open and I yelled after him that I'd be in touch.

I went back to staring at my timetables, waiting for an epiphany, but making no more headway than Carmody had made staring at the watches. I began to think that I should pay a visit to the Widow

Dwinn, the oracle of all things train, for some enlightenment.

Maybe she would enlighten me as to why railroads were being robbed and sabotaged, and whether robbers had anything to gain from the sabotage, why they would do it, and why on earth a member of a gang who may or may not have something to do with the incidents had lost his watch during the massacre of a peaceful settlement, a massacre perpetrated by a cult of lunatics who lived the next town over.

My frustration level was so great that I welcomed the distraction of the scuffle I heard escalating outside.

I'd been aware of increasingly angry words being exchanged for a couple minutes, but put off dealing with the dustup because I anticipated my stroke of genius arriving at any moment.

But life is full of disappointments.

So I put my hand on my revolver and consoled myself with the fact that I'd soon be able to club somebody who deserved it upside the head.

When there's trouble, I don't walk directly in or out of a door. I usually open it from the side, and then poke my head in, making damn sure I'm prepared to retract it like a turtle if somebody wants to shoot it off.

My door was standing open, but I still approached it from the side and peeked around the frame.

Liddicoat was squared off, about ten feet away, with a muscular blond man I didn't know. To the side stood two other men I'd never seen before, both dressed in vested suits, sash ties, one sporting a beard and the other wearing tiny round spectacles.

Liddicoat was stiff with anger.

The blond man taunted him with a casual grin and flexed his fingers above the butt of his pistol.

The blond man then spit, and while it didn't carry anywhere near the ten feet separating them the intent was clear, and Liddicoat, enraged, went for his gun.

Liddicoat was practiced and fast. His movements were compact and he wasted no time or motion almost clearing the holster.

The tip of the barrel was about to emerge by the time the blond man drew and shot him twice.

The blond man had reholstered before Liddicoat pitched to the ground, face-first.

He landed with a splash. Even after two sunny days, the street was still wet.

Chapter 49

The gunman had seen me, and he was smart. Reholstering the gun, in front of witnesses, would make it difficult for me to start shooting and then somehow claim justification.

At that moment I didn't want to shoot anybody before I found out what the hell was going on.

I walked up to them slowly, and the one with the flowing gray beard said: "Who the hell are you?"

It takes a lot to surprise me, but that did it.

"Who the hell am *I?* You're standing over a dead body and you ask who *I am?* Let's start with you."

Graybeard shrugged and raised his eyebrows, as though indulging a temperamental child.

"All right, if you must. I'm Amasa Pratt. This is John Grout. We're attorneys, and we came here to serve cease and desist papers against this man for harassment of our client. And everything we've heard is apparently true because without provocation he drew a weapon."

I turned to the blond man. He wore a hat but I could see that the sides of his head of hair were long and combed back in yellow coils. He wasn't tall, maybe 5' 8", but very broad through the chest and you could see the round bulge of the caps of his shoulders, like small cannonballs, underneath a bright blue shirt.

"And you?" I asked the blond man.

"Henry Best."

He said it plainly as though it meant something to me, which of course it did.

Pratt, the bearded one, had something to say and wanted it on the record.

"We came here to lawfully execute a civil matter. We have associates in Austin who know we are coming and will expect us to return and will immediately pursue a remedy if we're not back. Knowing the proclivity of the town marshal to gratuitous violence we hired Mr. Best for protection."

Grout was preparing to speak. He tilted his head back and opened his mouth as though his words would carry such force he needed to allow them an easy escape route.

"A badge doesn't give a hoodlum any special license to kill," Grout said, speaking slowly and mechanically, as through reciting from a memorized script. "And we know that the late Mr. Hawke was appointed through dubious means to begin with."

The late Mr. Liddicoat had graciously eaten a bullet intended for me, but I wasn't ready to let them know that.

Chapter 50

"There's an ordinance against carrying firearms in the town limits," I said. It might have actually been true. Like most towns on the frontier, laws in Shadow Valley were written, rewritten, forgotten and written again. My filing cabinet had ordinances, resolutions, and proclamations dating back twenty-five years, many signed by people who were no longer here and in some cases no longer remembered by even the most long-time current residents.

There was an ordinance against carrying firearms dated before the war, likely unenforceable from a practical and legal standpoint, but I trotted it out when it served my purpose.

Pratt started jawing me and that gray beard moved up and down like a piston.

"There's no notice of that," he said. You can't enforce a law that's not posted. And you can't selectively enforce an ordinance. We saw plenty of folks carrying."

There were only a few people on the street; most, fearing trouble, had rabbited inside. But in a few moments someone with a spine would sidle up and there could be gunplay.

I had to make some decisions quickly, and my options were limited.

I was pretty sure Pratt and Grout were real lawyers. No one can become that wordy by accident.

They were hired by Carpenter ostensibly to seek legal recourse for the death of his henchmen but were really here to legitimize my murder. Two lawyers prepared to swear that Henry Best was acting in self-defense.

For the time being, they had me checkmated. I couldn't throw them all in jail because they'd already threatened me with backup brigades of lawyers if they didn't return.

But that was secondary to the practical matter that Henry Best would never allow that, and that's why he was here.

Best was untouchable, too, because if I killed him I'd have two lawyers steering me to jail and if I killed the lawyers too I'd have their backups marching me to the gallows.

And there remained the formidable problem that I'd never seen anyone draw that fast.

I was checkmated.

Luckily for me, though, I was dead.

Chapter 51

Best stuck a finger in my chest so hard I could feel him push me off balance.

"You're the deputy, Carmody, right?"

I said nothing.

"Hawke here was a friend of yours, I guess," Best said, and lifted the chin of the corpse out of the mud with the toe of his boot.

"There's an ordinance prohibiting firearms within the town limits," I said.

Best didn't like that. He expected me to get mad because I was dead at his feet and he was mistreating my corpse.

Sometimes I can't help the thoughts that stroll through my head at inappropriate moments but it occurred to me that even though there was no law called "assault by horse," there *was* a state law against mistreating a corpse. Those words exactly: "mistreating a corpse."

He let what he thought was my face fall back into the mud.

Pratt and Grout didn't like what I'd said, either. It was a complication. Not much, but I'd loosened one of the little strings in the case they thought they'd tied up in advance.

"And where exactly are the town limits?" Pratt asked.

Actually, I didn't know. Nobody knew. Nobody cared. But I made something up about the stream near the bank to the north and the east-west trail to the south and the limits of the scrub land in back of the Silver Spoon and the other bar in town, the Full Moon.

Best wasn't stupid, and I was sorry to see that.

He began with the finger again.

"Just a short walk north of the bank," he said. "Maybe you want to finish what he started."

And he kicked Liddicoat – a.k.a. me – in the side of the head.

Hard. I heard a crack and a sucking sound as the force of the kick lifted the head out of the mud.

And then I saw Oak the blacksmith turn the corner.

He'd heard the shot and was coming over to help, right out in the open, *right down the center of the goddamn street.*

He wasn't even armed. He came striding in plain sight equipped with nothing but his muscles and his do-gooder determination to get all of us killed in a about five seconds if I didn't think of something.

"Are you aware," I asked Best, "that there is a state law against mistreating a corpse?"

Best mugged an expression meant to convey his disbelief in my abject idiocy and he let his jaw drop a little as he looked over at the roving law firm of Pratt and Grout with mean merriment in his eyes.

You never want to let you jaw hang like that. It's rude, you look stupid, and if you don't keep it shut and anchored to your shoulder, a punch to the point of the chin is likely to put you out cold, and it did.

Chapter 52

Pratt and Grout were at a loss for words, and I considered that an accomplishment.

Pratt finally sputtered something about assault and I fired back with what I thought was a very eloquent argument that I'd stopped the crime of mistreating a corpse and Grout began to stutter and Best started to twitch and flop and make mewling sounds the way they do when you really ring their bell and Oak stared at me and was about to ask why I was standing in my undershirt with a dead body in front of me in the mud so I shot Oak a glance and tiny shake of my head to let him know not to say anything and then I yelled for everybody to shut up.

They all did, except for Best, who kept mewling and twitching like he was getting bit by ants.

I told Pratt to bring all three of their horses over.

I took Best's gun and Oak and I loaded him onto his horse, laying him across the saddle, and lashed him in place with some rope I had in the office. I never could have done it single-handed; Best was astonishingly heavy for someone so squat.

Oak tied the lead of Best's horse to the pommel of Pratt's mount.

I told them to go away and stay away.

And I told them to tell Carpenter the same thing.

Pratt looked back several times, apprehensively, but gained courage as he reached the limits of shouting distance.

"You'll regret this, Carmody," he said, and they spurred away about as quickly as they could with the horse tethered to Pratt's saddle.

Oak started to ask me the obvious question but they could still hear us so I held up my hand before he could speak.

Chapter 53

Carmody, Elmira, and I met in her back room.
I'd changed back into my shirt, which was now cleaned and pressed as sharp a general's dress uniform; Elmira had even scraped the mud off my badge, polished it, and re-pinned it.

I'd stuck my left hand into a burlap bag filled with wet sawdust, which is what Elmira uses this time of year to keep the beer cool. Ice is scarce expensive around here in late September; what's been stored has long since melted or been used up and you can buy ice harvested from caves but the nearest ones are a long ride and it's not worth the effort or expense.

My hand throbbed but it wasn't broken and in a way the ache was comforting. I'd landed very few left hooks with that authority and I don't mind admitting that I was happy to see that I still had some steam in my boiler.

Carmody started the meeting with another hat-in-hand *mea culpa* and explaining Dorothea and he were both making up for lost time and then by the grace of God Elmira cut him off before he got specific and told him that things had worked out for the best.

Carmody didn't follow.

"Look," Elmira said, "if it had come to shooting, Carpenter had you both ways. If you lost, you'd be dead in a minute. If you won, you'd be dead in a week when they hanged you."

Carmody nodded, convinced.

In her moments of clarity Elmira has a succinct and quick way of summing things up, and I told her as much, leaving out the first, qualifying part of that statement.

"My mind works very fast," she said. "When I think of something I say it. And sometimes my mind works so fast I say it before I even *think* of it."

But her moments of clarity are often widely separated.

I told Carmody how the shooting had gone down and how Best and the lawyers assumed I was dead and that I was Carmody.

I had to explain it a couple times because even I got it tangled up.

We sat and stared at the table. Carmody was apparently thinking about how the assumption that I was dead could be turned to our advantage before somebody set Best and the lawyers straight.

I was pondering the philosophical implications of how Elmira could say something before she thought of it but gave up when I started to get a headache.

"All right," Carmody said at last, "I get the part about Carpenter wanting to get back at you for killing his son. I get the part about the robberies.

And if Carpenter's behind all these robberies we been reading about, the fact that him and his son and some of his gang got them watches makes sense."

Elmira poured us all another drink – we'd gone back to the cheap stuff, which is just as well because the taste is so foul I'm not so tempted to overindulge – and we looked at our glasses for a while.

"So it makes some sense," she said, "that young Carpenter went off his rails when you showed up at the door with the watch. In his mind he probably assumed you were there to confront him with evidence of his involvement."

"I agree," I said. "But then things start to unravel. First, why did Nonie find the watch at the town massacre? How does that fit in? Second, when I talked with the Pink and the railroad bulls they told me there had been more than a hundred acts of vandalism in the last six months. Collisions and near-misses because of switch sabotage. Track torn up. And it's not just what was done but the *way* it was done. Timed and calculated for maximum damage. Somebody really put some thought into the process."

"But wouldn't that be part and parcel of smart train robbing?" Carmody asked, moving a shotglass to the left side of the table. "Stage a derailment here, and then when you get a whole passel of railroad bulls and Pinks and personnel on the scene, pull off a robbery... "

He pulled another shotglass off the shelf in back of him and set it down on the right side of the table.

"Here."

"It makes perfect sense," I said, "but that's not how it happened. That's what I was looking for with all those charts and timetables. The robberies, yes, a couple times it does look like one was staged in the aftermath of another."

Carmody casually refilled both shotglasses. I had suspected he was less in need of a visual aid and more concerned with a mechanism to drink more quickly.

Elmira looked up.

"Could they be separate groups? With different agendas? One likes to steal, and the other likes to break stuff?"

"Could be coincidence," I said. "It's a stretch, but strange, unconnected stuff does happen. That's why we have the word 'coincidence.'"

"Coincidences make me itch," Carmody said.

I told him I agreed.

"Maybe they's stealing for the money but using that money to pay for the gangs that break the stuff and try to kill marshals," Carmody said.

I shrugged.

"Why?" I asked. "That's benighted."

Carmody shook his head and poured another two drinks.

"Maybe they just plain hate railroads, like I hate people who use fancy words just to be *bellicose.*"

I acknowledged he'd winged me.

"Or *rebarbative,*" he added, solemnly.

"You win," I told him. "But you're being *obtuse*. Nobody hates railroads. Why would anybody hate a railroad?"

"Are you serious?" Elmira said.

She was incredulous, and looked at me as though I'd just dropped my pants.

"This is *Texas,*" she said, as though that explained it all.

Chapter 54

And when she finished with her story, it did explain it all.

I'd forgotten, if I ever knew, that her former husband had, among other enterprises, been involved in railroading.

Bannister Adler was involved in three lines that went bust but still managed to pocket a profit. There was a lot of money flowing into the rail system as Texas grew. Investment in railroads was viewed as essential throughout the history of the territory, then the republic, and what eventually was incorporated as the state.

Texas is huge, Elmira reminded me, though I needed no reminding.

There's no waterway system to speak of and the geography of the state features baking deserts, sweltering swamp, forbidding hills and dense forests.

As a result, town, cities, and counties took out bonds to fund private railroad developers, and the government went so far as to seize lands and grant them to rail lines. Unfortunately, railroad developers – at least in Elmira's version of events – had the morals of rattlesnakes and the financial acumen of doorknobs. Project after project folded, developers pocketed the spoils, and taxpayers and landowners provided the pockets.

Many regarded the railway system as a web of bribery, secret cartels, and political payback.

When a rail line actually materialized, there was enormous profit to be made by the chosen and connected few who acquired property along planned lines and opened warehouses, restaurants, hotels, and the like.

That's what almost happened to Elmira when the scrubland in back of the Spoon was slated as the site of a railroad line, and why people were willing to kill to take the property from her. We'd heard through channels that the route was changed because of some underhanded political wheeling and dealing. The shadow world of high-stakes deal-making conceals its plans in ulterior motives and covers them with coatings of lies, so you never know which layer of the onion is the one that's stinking the worst.

"So why would Carpenter have a hard-on for the railroads?" Carmody asked, and then remembered he was in polite company and smiled at Elmira.

"Excuse my trail talk."

"He hates railroads because he's a *rancher,*" she said.

"Meaning that the railroads screwed him out of his land," I translated.

Carmody jabbed a finger into the table.

"Well, shit, that makes sense. Him and his folk been around here for a long time, couple generations from what I've heard. And they was trappers before that. They been running their cattle on land and probably come to think they own as far as they can see."

"And we know they're crooks to boot," I said. "They've got fingers in every crooked pie from here to the Big Bend."

"Ain't no fury like a chiseler out-chiseled," Carmody said.

"And that explains why Old Man Carpenter called me a 'thieving squatter,'" I said. "I didn't pay it any mind because in my business people call you so many names it's hard to keep track."

"Josiah, you don't know the *half* of what they say about you," Elmira added.

She looked as though she wanted to elaborate but I figured it could wait.

Carmody was intent, on point, like when he's tracking.

I almost expected him to sniff the air and bark.

Instead, Carmody asked me why Best was involved in this. From the article Harbold had sent, it looked like Best was doing gunwork for the railroad people. Why would he take up the cause of an anti-railroad fanatic?

I knew the answer. I'd once been in pretty much the same business as Best for a while, before I became my present saintly self, but that was something I didn't talk much about, even to Carmody and Elmira.

"It makes absolutely no difference to him or anybody like him. He's a mercenary. A gun for hire to the highest bidder."

"I'm not sure I want to know the answer to this," Elmira said.

Carmody didn't circle around the tree very long once he'd cornered an idea.

"This leads us to what happened to Nonie," he said, stabbing his index finger into the table every time he ticked off a point. Why that watch was there. Why Carpenter and his boy were hooked with a bunch of crazies from the Church of the Divine Lunatic or whatever it was. Why they wiped out the town next door – hacking people into pieces, except for Nonie, who got away and had that vision of hell burnt into her mind so hot she can't talk no more."

I had a map back in the office and could get it in a minute, and I told them I'd fetch it.

"No need for you to start drawing pictures, Josiah. We all know the answer. Them mountain towns is all in the range of what Carpenter would call *his property*. The towns ain't no good for ranching, but maybe there's minerals and gems. I don't know. Or maybe it just don't matter if it weren't good for nothing at all because Carpenter *wanted it*. The land was *his*."

"He was in a blind rage," I said, fitting the pieces together as I said it. "And he found a cult to do his killing for him. Got them to raid the next town over and kill heretics. I always wondered where the money came from for cult members to live there, to build the houses, to put up that big church. It was always on my mind."

"And then," Carmody said, "he needed somebody to wipe out the cult."

I read in a pretty badly written book once how the "silence hung heavily in the air."

I thought it was a hackneyed phrase but maybe I did the author a disservice because now it was pretty real to me. I could almost literally *feel* the silence and it weighed me down like a mudslide.

As far as I know, almost everyone involved in the murderous cult, headed by a minister named Lobb in a place he psychotically named Lobbtown, was dead, in jail, in the case of the children, put up for adoption, and in the case of one of those children, picking up dirty glasses in a bar.

There was a clear swath of land up northwest of us now, running in an arc that stretched and dipped to connect with Carpenter's holdings closer to Shadow Valley and maybe ten miles to our west.

Carpenter now could make a fortune off his land after using a cult to kill townsfolk who'd been in his way.

And, to cover Carpenter's tracks, the cult had then been wiped out.

And Carmody and I were the ones who did it.

We'd finished up Carpenter's dirty work for him.

Chapter 55

I cowpoked up some Tchaikovsky, drawing it out and slowing it down until it would have somehow made the notoriously morose Tchaikovsky even more depressed, and talked strategy with Carmody.

"I think tomorrow they're going to come gunning for you," he said.

"Not me. *You.* I'm dead, remember?"

"Lucky you."

"They're setting us up."

"Setting *me* up," Carmody said. "And what do you mean?"

"This is about erasing anyone who can connect them to the robberies and sabotage and what happened in the mountain town. I don't think they're much interested in wiping out Shadow Valley, although I don't think their conscience would be bothered much.'"

"What about Nonie?"

"Can't say for sure," I said, "but I don't think they would even know about her."

"Elmira?"

"Can't say for sure, either, but I don't think they'd view her as an active threat. We're the ones pulling on the thread; we're the ones with the gun and badges. We're the ones who make their problems go away if we become dead."

"You sound convincing," Carmody said, "which is one reason why you're so dangerous. But I still don't get what you mean by being set up."

"I would guess that the last thing Carpenter wants is more entanglement with the law. He wants a neat case of self-defense, and he wants witnesses to tie the bows on that case. That's why Best goaded Liddicoat into drawing, and why there were two lawyers on hand taking notes. I half expected them to set up a camera like Matthew Brady and light some flash powder."

"So," Carmody said, "what the fuck do we do?"

"One of us should ride to Austin tomorrow and find Harbold or Munro and lay out the whole story. Get some constables and rangers down here. And maybe some of our own lawyers to stand around and take notes. We could send somebody else, like Miller or Oak, but this is a complicated problem and we're going to need to work some things out."

"Why not just wire them?"

"I thought about that," I said, "but unless I can learn Morse code by morning I have to involve that weasel at the telegraph office, and I think he's got wires running in directions we don't know about."

Carmody seemed uncharacteristically tense.

"Which one of us goes?"

"Maybe you," I said. "You're a better rider and the trails still aren't dry. Last time I almost sunk in quicksand."

"There ain't no quicksand anywhere around here. You was peeing yourself because you got stuck in plain old terrifying *mud*. And it sounds like you're sending me out of harm's way so I don't get hurt here if you ain't around to protect me."

"That never occurred to me," I lied. In most other life-and-death situations I'd give Carmody a better shot at survival than myself, but this was not his type of game.

But I told him that if he wanted to mind the fort, that was fine with me.

"Don't trust me to get the story straight with your fancy officer friends?"

Monroe had been a major in my unit. Harbold and I had been lieutenants. Unforgivable sins in the eyes of Sgt. Carmody.

"Nothing I say strikes you quite right tonight, does it?"

"It ain't that," Carmody said. "Just that this whole business stinks. We're the law but the law's been used against *us*. Everybody's got some connection, some sneaky back door, and nobody gives a rat's ass about right and wrong. Some guy working for the bank, that Liddicoat guy, probably just trying to make an honest living, well he's dead because he got in the way of another fucking railroad scheme."

I told him I agreed and kept quiet. When Carmody's set to give a monologue, there's not much to do except ride it out and applaud at the end.

"How come we can't make the law work on our side?" he said. "Why don't we just track them down and arrest them?"

"There's nothing I can charge them with," I said, "except mistreating a corpse."

I tried to distract him but it didn't work. He wasn't in the mood. He had something on his mind and was weighing how to say it.

"Why don't we just track them down and kill them?"

I shifted and took my time answering.

"Best will not kill easily. Neither will Carpenter, but this is Best's business and he's good at it."

"Meaning you're afraid Best will kill you," Carmody said, and it wasn't a question.

"Not me, *you*. Remember, I'm already dead."

Carmody nodded, small, thoughtful nods that persisted for a couple minutes while he stared straight ahead. I had no idea what he was thinking about. Maybe some brilliant strategy. Maybe that job he'd been offered in Copper Ridge that he hadn't bothered to tell me about. Or maybe he was just brooding about what a shitty day it had been.

"This has been a goddamn shitty day," he said, answering my question as he stood up and hitched his pants.

It gets worse, I said, reminding him about Liddicoat's body, which I'd stuffed into the corner of our office.

Tomorrow looked to be a hot one.

Chapter 56

Carmody and I agreed to meet before dawn at the Spoon. We didn't want to go to the office. It didn't smell all that great before, and now there was a new body decomposing there.

We set our meeting time at exactly 5:30 a.m.

All these fancy watches floating around were giving us a fetish about precise meeting times.

We never did come to an agreement on who would make the ride to Austin and deferred it until morning.

When I came down he'd already made a pot of coffee.

"You're late," he said. "It's 5:31."

"Sorry, I didn't sleep well."

"5:31 and fifteen seconds."

This promised to devolve into an endless back-and-forth, so I changed the subject.

"Want to flip a coin to see who makes the trip? One of us has to go and one of us has to stay. And I have no idea how they're going to come at us so it probably doesn't matter much."

"I'll go," Carmody said. "You're right. You might get lost or sink in the mud or see a scary spider in your path and have to turn around."

I was about to say something when we heard the hoofbeats.

Movement is pretty rare around here before dawn. In fact, in a place where most activity is centered around gambling and drinking, nothing much stirs until eleven.

"Single rider," Carmody said.

I opened the front door and didn't like what I saw.

Dorothea Dwinn was riding in at full gallop, wearing nightclothes and an expression of pure horror.

And then I noticed that the corners of the early-morning night sky were turning blood red.

Chapter 57

They'd burned her house down.

She didn't see any of them. All she heard was a sudden cacophony of hoofbeats, pounding on the door, the crackle of fire, and a voice at the window telling her that they'd kill her the next time unless "her man" did something about it.

Then a burning torch rocketed through the window and the voice said: "Dawn, north of the bank."

Dorothea was inconsolable. The house was likely all she had, other than the clothes on her back and the sorry horse she'd ridden into town.

I roughly and insistently woke Elmira to help take care of her.

Elmira was incomprehensible. She said words, or what I thought were words, and moved about, occasionally bumping into things, but was of no use for the moment.

Carmody was in a white-hot rage. He checked the loads in his revolver, re-holstered, and moved toward the door.

We all told him to stop.

Elmira snapped out of her delirium and said *stop,* clearly and in recognizable English. Her eyes were focused. I actually looked twice to reassure myself that I wasn't dreaming.

Dorothea wailed. *"Tommy, stop, please."* Desperation and misery contorted her face and she looked as vulnerable as a child. I'd seen that look before, and seeing it in Dorothea literally made my stomach hurt. It was the despair of people about to lose the last thing on earth they cared about.

"Stop," I said to Carmody, as softly as I could while still being heard over Dorothea's sobs.

"This is exactly what they want," I told him. "They found out Dorothea's your girl and did what they did to lure you outside the town limits and Best is going to stage it so they can say you drew on him."

"So *what.*" Carmody spat the words. It wasn't a question.

"It's his game," I said. "You *can't win.* He's got you thinking crazy and acting crazier."

Carmody must have known I was right. He must have understood that there were alternatives. We could try to ambush them, although I imagine they'd be prepared for that. We could mount a charge, maybe with Oak and Miller, and sort out the legal questions later, though maybe we'd be doing it on our way to the gallows.

Carmody must have also understood that the only *good* alternative was to let me play this hand out. Go through the whole insane ritual of the goddamned fair draw. If I won, Carmody could use that buffalo gun to make sure there was no funny business.

If I lost…well, that would be a circumstance beyond my control, so he'd have to figure it out.

But I'd seen Best draw. I'd seen few as good and none better.

I might win. I might not.

Carmody could not win.

I was about to try to explain all that when he shoved past me.

Chapter 58

I grabbed Carmody by the shoulder.

"Don't do it," I said.

He shook me off and I grabbed him again.

"This isn't your kind of fight," I said.

"Don't you be telling me what I can and cannot do."

"Don't play into their hands," I said. "You can't go."

"Who's stopping me?"

"I am," I said, and stepped in front of the door.

Chapter 59

Carmody took me by the shirt and twisted me away from the door.

I went along with it and stepped down with my left leg in back of his left knee and then jerked my leg straight. His knee buckled and I was able to throw him down.

He tucked his head to avoid hitting it on the floor but not before he'd exposed his throat long enough for me to kill him with a thrust to his Adam's apple.

I didn't, of course, and there lay the problem. I was trying to keep him from being killed and couldn't very well kill him in the process.

And there lay the futility of all conflict. We want to hurt people, we *need* to hurt people sometimes, but usually not too much. Maybe we hold back for practical reasons, like not wanting to kill the idiot we're trying to save. Other times it's out of fear of repercussions and escalation. I'd feel no qualms about climbing a tree and putting a bullet in Carpenter's brain, for example, but I knew that would be the first step to a meeting with the hangman.

And sometimes it's a matter of right and wrong and the elusive nature of figuring it all out. Like the times I chose not to kill rebs and took them prisoner instead, even knowing that they would kill me given a chance. Or when I was chasing a suspect and he ducked into a church and I waited the whole day for him to come out.

There are some lines you don't cross.

I was wondering where Carmody, who until a minute ago was my best friend, would draw his lines after he regained his footing.

Chapter 60

He bull-rushed me, head down.

Normally you grab for a headlock, go with the motion, fall on your back, and pull the man over your head. But Carmody was too strong. I had a lock on his neck but he lifted me off my feet and kept charging until I hit the wall.

Elmira and Dorothea screamed.

It looked and sounded a lot worse than it was. I hit flat and wasn't hurt much because I spread the impact across my legs and back, but the force was terrific and things fell off shelves and I heard the wall crack behind me.

Carmody wrapped his hands around my back and lifted me in the air.

He was going to ram me into the wall again and there was nothing I could do to stop his momentum.

So I slapped him on the ears with the palms of my hands, bringing them together violently on each side of his head.

I didn't want to do that – it hurts like hell and you can do some serious damage to the ears – but I was afraid that he was going to put me through the wall. Literally.

He did manage to slam me but his stride was off and he was disoriented by the blow. Getting hit in the ear, for reasons I don't understand, affects your balance and he was staggered.

He fell back a couple steps, his hands down.

I saw an opportunity to end it with the same left hook I'd used to flatten Henry Best.

It landed perfectly, and I could fell the force of the blow emanating all the way up from the balls of my feet. I put everything behind it, and it was the best hook I'd ever landed.

Carmody shook his head, like you shake a watch when it stops, and charged me again.

Chapter 61

I tried kneeing him as he came in and I connected to the forehead but it didn't slow him down much.

He had me in the same position again, his head in my chest, and was actually digging his head in and lifting me like a bull.

I realized that this time he really was going to put me through the wall. What was left of me after, assuming I survived, would be powerless to stop him from getting himself killed.

I had a decision to make.

I could stop him by interlacing my fingers and bringing the weight of my hands down on the back of his neck.

That would stop him. It could also paralyze him and quite possibly kill him. There's no way to gauge the effects of a blow like that. Too soft and he wouldn't even feel it. Too hard and his neck would be broken.

It was all or nothing at all.

I was still contemplating the back of his neck when Elmira laid Carmody out cold with one of those goddamned brass candlesticks.

Chapter 62

I was hurt more than I expected and I wobbled when I walked.

Dorothea rushed to Carmody, who was spread-eagled, and cradled his head in her hands.

She pulled up his eyelid and let it close again. It wasn't the first time she'd dealt with an injured man, obviously.

She felt the back of his head and her hand came away bloody but not soaked.

"I think he'll be all right," she said, her voice quavering so violently I had trouble understanding her.

I leaned on a chair as the room spun around me.

"Dorothea," I said, "if you love Tom I need you to do exactly what I say."

She nodded and I handed her the keys to my office.

"In my desk, bottom left drawer, there's a pair of handcuffs. They have a hinge and a ratchet. Stick the prong in the end and tighten them up. You're good with stuff like that. You'll know what to do. Put one around Carmody's wrist and one on the bar-rail. You'll have to drag him a few feet to reach it but you and Elmira can do it."

I noticed that Carmody's eyes were flickering.

"*Hurry.*"

There was some water left in a sink behind the bar and I splashed my face with it.

Elmira walked over and set the candlestick down, deliberately, from where she'd picked it up.

"It has to be like this," she said, "doesn't it?"

"Yes."

"You're hurt."

"I am, but I'm moving all right. I'll come back to my senses soon."

She just looked at me.

"So let me do what I need to do," I told her, "before I get my sanity back."

Carmody was still out. Dorothea would need another minute to get the cuffs and scuttle back to the Spoon.

It was just Elmira and me, and there was nothing to say. Nothing we needed to say.

I looked in her eyes and realized that I was peering into an infinite well of resilience.

I've seen more than my share of phony tough guys. They give you the stony eyeball in the beginning but when things begin to hurt their eyes plead with you to make it stop.

Some people talk tough. Dorothea can swear and spit with the best of them but down deep she's civilized and delicate – nothing wrong with that –

and she was shaken to the bone by what happened to her house and then to Tom.

Any normal person would be.

Elmira was not a normal person anymore.

She'd lost everything more than once. She'd seen real bloodshed and lived a hard life among the Apaches and while she could be sensitive and caring and not immune to bouts of crying when the spirit moved her, at the core of her soul she knew the way the world worked.

Her eyes had gone hard with her hatred of people who hated for no reason, her hatred of people who preyed on others.

I think she wanted to say goodbye just in case but knew that any scene now would delay me.

She also knew that the very last thing either of us needed was for me to be distracted by thoughts of love, attachment, loss, or other elements of the normal world that was inhabited by normal people.

I adjusted my rig and made sure my sidearm hadn't been damaged in the fight. It happens more often than you'd expect. There's been a lot of slamming going around and it's easy to get your barrel bent.

I was going to say something but all I could do was look at her and notice how beautiful she was, how her beauty was like a fireplace or a fine painting – she was always the focal point in every room and everything in the environment seemed to arrange itself around her.

There was nothing I could say, so I turned and walked away.

"Josiah," she said, as I stepped onto the boardwalk.

"Yes?"

"*Kill him.*"

Chapter 63

Best was alone in a clearing just a little north of our mythical town border.

I knew he wasn't really alone, that there would be backup in the woods, and I told him as much.

He shrugged.

"Don't worry about nobody else, Carmody. I'm your problem."

"And I'm not Carmody." I told him the story, about how he'd killed some guy who just happened to be in the wrong place at the wrong time, and that I, Josiah Hawke, had just come back from the dead to haunt him.

"Don't matter to me if you call yourself Ulysses S. Grant," Best said. "I'll kill you if you draw on me."

"I know you're playing to the audience behind the trees, Best. Setting this up so you can say it was a fair fight."

"*Carpenter,*" I shouted. "I know you're out there. And here's how it's going to go down."

There was nothing but the sound of the wind in the trees. It was brisk and picking up; the sky was red and on the horizon I could see flashes of lighting.

"I have people in this town to protect," I shouted to the trees. "Some are good people. Very good people. Some are assholes. But it's my job to protect them, anyway."

Best began shifting his weight from leg to leg.

"Either way it's over," I said. "If Best kills me, there's no one left to follow up on this train stuff. My deputy's dumber than a box of rocks and all he does is collect taxes and clean the guns. So leave him alone."

There was a rumble of thunder and I heard a drop of rain hit the brim of my hat.

"If I kill Best, I'm ending it myself. I'm not coming after you. I don't care about this train business and I *never* did. *Never!* All I wanted to do was give your son his goddamned watch back."

I squared myself to Best and took a couple paces back. The wind picked up even more and I could hear the cloth of Best's sleeves snapping.

"I know you've got a bunch of witnesses in there," I yelled, feeling the rain in my face. "After the smoke clears, you can go to court if you want to and everybody will say it was a fair fight and that I'd said you're not involved in any criminality."

I thought I heard some movement but couldn't be sure.

"I've got people here, too," I lied, "so after I kill your boy, if it works out that way, don't get any ideas. Everybody just packs up and leaves and that's the end of it. No more shooting. No more."

"You talk a lot," Best said.

"Time for talk is over," I said.

He flashed a mirthless grin and gave me the stony eyeball.

Chapter 64

In any sort of fighting, you're usually better off keeping your emotions out of it. They cloud your thinking and impair your strategy. Generally, you waste a lot of energy flailing away, fueled by your hatred, when you should be striking with economy and precision.

Then there comes a time when rage is your friend. You blood pumps and your focus narrows and every particle in your body and soul aligns behind the goal of killing.

Best was smiling, no doubt to taunt me and goad me into making a move.

Despite what you read in the dime novels, there's no real etiquette in a draw. Nobody waits for the other person to move first nor is there any way to prove who made the first move.

Oh, it'll be hashed out in court, all right. Ten people will say one thing and ten will say the opposite. The judge will decide based on intuition, which witness he owes the most favors to, or whoever gave him the biggest bribe.

Nor does the first person to draw always win. Quick-draw artists put on good street shows but they rarely win gunfights. First shots can miss, or fail to kill, and the outcome is decided not by the first bullet but the last one that hits where it counts.

Best gave a little laugh and I thought I saw his hand move.

It doesn't really matter now who moved first.

I put two shots in his chest before he was able to clear the holster.

Rage had been my friend this morning.

Chapter 65

He stiffened and fell straight back, his gun still pointed at his foot, but I didn't watch long enough to see him hit the grass.

I flattened myself and scanned the trees.

They could be anywhere. I was only a hundred feet away from the ruined bank building, and there could have been a hundred people in there for all I knew, but the woods in back of the clearing seemed like the most likely hiding spot. It was elevated and there were several trails running through the woods just a few hundred feet farther up.

I rolled, moving toward a gentle slope where the landscape would provide me a little cover.

A bullet slapped into the damp grass to my left and I heard the crack of a rifle.

I could see the sturdy silhouette of Carpenter as he moved toward me.

He was no stranger to gunplay. I'd caught him by surprise when I hit the deck like that, knowing that he'd never let me walk away, but he still came pretty close with a shot on a barely visible, moving target.

Carpenter knew that he had the drop on me, no matter how good a shot I was with a pistol. A rifle carries twice as far and has twice the accuracy. My rifle was back in the office, a quarter mile away.

It might as well have been in Arizona.

Carpenter began advancing. As far as I could see he was alone. I imagine that he'd brought along a couple witnesses, probably the lawyers, but I also could see the logic in not inviting a crowd. More tongues to wag. And he'd assumed that Best would kill me. And if Best didn't kill me, Carpenter figured he'd finish me off while I admired my work and then he would melt back into the trails.

I fired a shot just to keep him occupied, ran in a zig-zag toward the bank and then hit the ground again.

My only chance was to get to the cover of the bank building that was sitting sideways near the road.

I calculated that at this rate I'd get there in about a week.

Meanwhile, Carpenter was striding purposefully toward me, knowing that he could hit me and I stood very little chance of reaching him.

I'd considered the possibility that one of his men might have holed up in the bank but dismissed it.

Then I heard the roar of a big-bore rifle in back of me and wished I'd run in the opposite direction.

And then, oddly, I heard nothing.

In the distance, Carpenter turned a half circle and fell.

I scrambled to my back and saw Carmody standing on top of the bank building, lowering his rifle.

From his left wrist dangled my new W.V. Adams patented ratcheting handcuffs, and from the other cuff danged at least six feet of shiny brass bar rail, bent and dented and torn. Dorothea had fastened it pretty tight and the metal joints at both ends were too big to fit through the opening of the handcuff.

"As soon as my head stops hurting," Carmody said, "we gotta have a talk about that 'dumb as a bag of rocks' remark."

Chapter 66

Dorothea clapped her hands with glee, told me it was great that I wasn't dead, and ordered another round.

It was hard for me to disagree with the sentiment.

Nonie silently glided up to the table, filled our glasses, and deposited a lighted candle on the table.

"I am sorry about crowning you with that thing," Dorothea said, and Elmira and I tried to avoid looking at her or each other.

"I think that's the one I used," Dorothea said. "It's bent."

Taking the rap for Carmody's rap on the head was Dorothea's idea, a gesture of gratitude for Elmira and I keeping Carmody from facing inevitable perforation if he drew with Best. Elmira would have fessed up, reluctantly, but was more than happy to play along in the ruse.

And I have to admit Dorothea found a great way for everyone to save face, except me. As she was on her fifth or sixth round, she delighted in retelling her story.

"I knew he was your best friend, Tommy. And he was only trying to help. But you was going to *kill* him."

"I don't remember the exact moment of being hit," Carmody said. "When you're put out cold, you never do, but I do remember tossing Josiah around like a rag doll before you brained me."

"He was *begging* for help toward the end, weren't he, Elmira? It was just pitiful. I couldn't stand to see my Tommy snap your man like a wishbone."

Elmira kept her gaze fixed on the candle.

"It still gives me chills," Elmira said. "Maybe we shouldn't talk about it anymore."

"Good idea," Carmody said. "It's over. No reason to feel bad. Weren't Josiah's kind of fight, that's all."

Dorothea did not have an off switch.

"And you would have out-drew that gun-fighter anyway."

"No," Carmody said, "I would not."

And then the conversation died and I turned to the piano.

I could hear the wind wailing. The red sky had given way to another storm. But it looked like this one would soon pass.

I kept the volume down so we could still converse, but I planned to pound away if the talk turned back to how I'd begged for mercy.

"Wow, you can play real soft," Dorothea said, downing another shot and wiping her chin with the back of her hand. I noticed that there was still a trail of whiskey dribbling down and she somehow managed to miss wiping part of that huge chin. She was really lit.

"Tommy says you told him the word *piano* means soft," Dorothea slurred.

"It was originally called *pianoforte*," I said. "That means *soft-loud* in Latin. It replaced the harpsichord, which only played at one volume."

Dorothea clapped her hands again.

"That's really *something*. Tommy says you know a heap of stuff. And he says you is always going off on some lecture nobody wants to hear about stuff nobody cares nothing about and everybody's too afraid a you to put a stop to it."

Carmody cleared his throat and showed a sudden interest in the ceiling.

I played louder.

Dorothea spoke louder.

"Tommy says he's afraid to ask you what time it is because you'll tell him how to build a watch."

"Speaking of watches," Carmody said quickly, some urgency in his voice as he changed the subject, "what about Carpenter and his gang? You think we'll hear any more from them?"

I decided to do some talking, regardless of how tedious certain people may find it, so I segued to some very soft Mozart.

"I think Carpenter's issues died with Carpenter," I said. "I don't think we'll hear from his lawyers or his witnesses hiding in the woods, if there were any. Maybe the train robberies and vandalism will go on. Probably will. There will always be a need for new Carpenters."

Elmira took her eyes off the candle and snapped to attention.

"That's a strange way to put it. 'A need for new Carpenters.' What does that mean?"

"I suppose Texas is like everywhere else," I said. "You've got people in secret pulling strings, and above them there are even more shadowy people pulling *their* strings. People like Carpenter are tools to them. They fire them up. Feed off their heat."

"I still don't follow," Elmira said.

"*Rage.* Rage is a commodity. Lots of people feel it because they think they've been cheated and wronged, like Old Man Carpenter. And maybe he was, but I think somebody was stoking him. Using him."

"For what?" Carmody said.

"I don't know where the thread ends," I admitted. "But railroads are a business that accounts for millions of dollars and a decision to have or *not to have* a railroad in one particular place can make or break fortunes. And don't forget about the millions that have been poured into the industry by governments – state, local, and federal – that have been stolen, lost, or unaccounted for, and are without a doubt lining many pockets."

"So you think somebody was using Carpenter?" Elmira said.

"Maybe," I said. "Lots of people use lots of other people. Carpenter used Best to get to me. To us. What sort of rage did Best have bottled up? Nobody goes into the business of killing unless there's something eating him alive."

I stopped playing and swiveled around on the bench to face them.

"Rage," I said. "Mindless, free-floating rage. Repackaged, bottled, and sold by politicians and crooks and the considerable intersection between those two groups."

Dorothea leaned on her elbows.

"And what are *you* so mad about, Josiah?"

She was trying to be funny. She was, as Carmody likes to put it, thoroughly cucumbered after downing damn near a full bottle all by herself.

When the conversation died Dorothea looked around the table, mystified, like the good-natured dog who chewed up a pair of shoes and doesn't understand why his owner isn't enjoying the game.

"What's the matter?" she said.

"You asked the universal question," Carmody said, in a suddenly festive tone, stabbing that huge index finger in the air. "And the answer is that we live in hard and stirring times."

He looked at me and waved at the piano.

"Ain't that right, Maestro?"

I gladly followed his lead, anxious to leave Dorothea's question hanging.

"You heard the first couple stanzas before the big storm and all the other shit that came down on us," I said, pecking out an introduction as I played.

"It's called, 'And That's What's the Matter,'" I said. "Stephen Foster wrote it during the War. The Union troops loved it, and sang it all the time in camps. But I'm not much of a singer."

"But I certainly am," Carmody said, and then he *stood on his chair.* He was as cucumbered as his girlfriend. And now he was singing from about nine feet in the air.

> *We live in hard and stirring times,*
> *Too sad for mirth, too rough for rhymes;*
> *For songs of peace have lost their chimes,*
> *And that's what's the matter!*

As often happens, people's accents disappear when they sing. Carmody sang like a operatic tenor in a concert hall, in a stunningly clear and ringing voice. I'd heard him sing before, but never belting it out at full throttle like he was tonight.

> *Oh! Yes, we thought our neighbors true,*
> *Indulg'd them as their mothers do;*
> *They storm'd our bright red, white and blue,*
> *And that's what's the matter!*
> *We'll never give up what we gain,*
> *For now we know we must maintain*
> *Our laws and rights with might and main;*
> *And that's what's the matter.*

The rest of the bar was as astonished as I. Jaws dropped. One grizzled old man actually dropped his glass on the floor.

The rebels thought we would divide,
And democrats would take their side;
They then would let the union slide,
And that's what's the matter!

And then a few of them joined in the singing. And then a few more. Around these parts war ditties are a risky proposition because you never know who was on which side, but sometimes the combination of music and alcohol and the cold remains of left-over anger can unite, rather than divide.

But, when the war had once begun,
All party feeling soon was gone;
We join'd as brothers, ev'ry one!
And that's what's the matter!

Epilogue

I had a terrific hangover the next morning but there were things to be tended to in the office.

I saw the envelope as soon as I opened the door.

The desk had been completely cleared and the envelope was precisely centered in the center of the oak rectangle.

It was addressed to me in Carmody's surprisingly florid cursive.

It occurred to me that Carmody didn't sing with an accent nor did he write with one. When he wrote something in the course of business, it was oddly baroque and formal.

I didn't want to read the letter. It was folded into thirds and when I lifted back the top I saw that it was dated and even affixed with a time.

I'd come to fucking hate those railroad watches.

The top of the letter read:

September 30, 1877
6:55 and 22 seconds a.m.
To: Marshal Josiah Hawke
From: Deputy Thomas Carmody

Re: My Employment with Shadow Valley

I took a deep breath and folded back the letter to see the bottom two-thirds.

Dear Marshal Hawke:

As I am sure you are aware, I have been offered a position as marshal of Copper Ridge.

I say that I am sure you are aware because your spit was still wet on the flap of the envelope from when you tried to re-seal it.

You are probably wondering why I did not mention this to you.

It's because I wanted to keep you in suspense and make you sweat for reading my mail.

But anyway, I am not interested in the job. Dorothea and I did take a ride out there just for the fun of it and I nosed around and about every fourth person is named Carpenter.

It is pretty obvious that the people there are part of this whole railroad scheme and the reason they offered me the job was to lure me away from Shadow Valley so that they could get to you. They know you need me around to protect what Taza calls "your sorry ass."

And on that note I have gone to bury that rotting body in the corner because I know you cannot do it because you are the sensitive type.

I will be back by lunch and you can buy.

Yours Sincerely,
Thomas Carmody
Deputy

THE END

About the Author

Carl Dane is a career journalist and author who has written more than 20 nonfiction books, hundreds of articles, and a produced play. He's worked as a television anchor and talk show host, newspaper columnist, and journalism professor.

He was born in San Antonio, Texas, and has maintained a lifelong interest in the Old West and the Civil War. He is a member of The Sons of Union Veterans and has traced many of ancestors not only to the Civil War, but also to the War of 1812 and the American Revolution.

Carl often writes and lectures about ethical dilemmas, and has a deep interest in morality, including questions of whether the ends justify the means and how far a reasonable person can go in committing an ostensibly wrong act to achieve a "greater good."

He has testified on ethical issues before the U.S. Congress and has appeared on a wide variety of television programs, including Fox News' *The O'Reilly Factor*, *ABC News World News Now*, *CBS Capitol Voices*, and CNN's *Outlook*.

Carl is also interested in the structure of effective and eloquent communication, and has written two recent books on professional writing and speaking for a commercial academic and reference publisher.

Reviewers have consistently praised his work for its deft humor.

When not coyly writing about himself in the third person, Carl lives in suburban New Jersey, where he is active in local government and volunteer organizations. He is the father of two sons.

The characters of Josiah Hawke and Tom Carmody – and the situations they confront – were drawn from the author's interest in the darker sides of the human soul, and the contradictions built into the psyche of every man and woman.

Hawke is an intellectual, a former professor of philosophy, who became drawn to the thrill of violence after the life-changing events of the Civil War – which not only exposed Hawke to violence but showed him that he possessed considerable untapped skill in that area. Carmody, yin to Hawke's yang, is a blunt backwoodsman who is no stranger to violence, either, but has fought for survival and not for sport. Carmody wonders if Hawke's philosophical justifications are merely a smokescreen for seeking out trouble – and he's not afraid to tell that to Hawke.

Follow Carl at www.carldane.com